T0131646

Joy

Joy

And 52 Other
Very Short Stories

Erin McGraw

Counterpoint
Berkeley, California

JOY

Library of Congress Cataloging-in-Publication Data
Names: McGraw, Erin, 1957– author.
Title: Joy : and 52 other very short stories / Erin McGraw.
Description: First hardcover edition. | Berkeley,
    California : Counterpoint, 2019.
Identifiers: LCCN 2018039857 | ISBN 9781640092082
Classification: LCC PS3563.C3674 A6 2019 | DDC
    813/.54—dc23
LC record available at https://lccn.loc.gov/2018039857

Paperback ISBN: 978-1-64009-352-2

Jacket design by Nicole Caputo
Book design by Wah-Ming Chang

COUNTERPOINT
2560 Ninth Street, Suite 318
Berkeley, CA 94710
www.counterpointpress.com

Printed in the United States of America

For Andrew

Now the days of riches are gone
and no one can bring them back for us.

But we can let ourselves be poor again.

—RAINER MARIA RILKE

Contents

Contents

Contents

Joy

America

Mr. Bixby is showing us again how to do the lay-back. He says we're all too stiff, but what he means is that we're all too white. *"Curl* your upper backs! With every kick you're *giving yourselves."* He kicks as high as his shoulder and lets his upper back droop and he looks idiotic, but he's trying to get Melissa Ridge to quit it with her ramrod ballet kicks, and anyway, Mr. Bixby is Mr. *West Side Story,* and all we can do is go along.

He's already got us, the Sharks and their girls, training with the Spanish teacher to improve our accents. He's training the Jets' accents himself, and now Trent Boynton, who's playing Action, goes around muttering, "Kick da can to da koib." If Trent runs into any of the Sharks, he's supposed to refuse to talk. Mr. Bixby won't let the Sharks and the Jets eat lunch together or hang out after school. "This isn't just a play," Mr. Bixby says. "It's a life." The day I woke up surprised to see my regular room and not a tenement, I told him about it. "That's—good, that's real good," he told me. I wasn't five feet away when he complained to Rob, the script boy he always keeps nearby, "We've been rehearsing for two months. What has she been doing?"

I've been learning to be Puerto Rican. At first I wanted to be Velma, Riff's girl, but Mr. Bixby cast Antoinette Mercer, who's so stupid that she can say her line—"Oublee-oo"—and sound like she means it. Now I'm Marisol, the name Mr. Bixby gave me, and I'll have leeway to improvise lines once Mr. Bixby thinks my accent is good enough.

First, though, I have to learn the steps to "America." It's an all-girl number, which I thought would make the dancing easy, but Mr. Bixby says we're supposed to dance in Spanish, and none of us knows how to do that. At first he told us to wiggle, but now he's telling us to ripple. "You can't just jiggle your skirt and think you're going to look Puerto Rican," he says, holding his hands up as if he were shaking out a towel. In case anybody has missed it, he's gay. "Your whole body is alive and flashing. The Jets girls are wound tight, but you are *exploding!*"

We try to explode. Some of the shows we've done are stupid—nobody has forgotten that cowbell in *Oklahoma!*— but I can feel *West Side Story*'s angular music scraping at my brain, its constant anger keeping me buzzing like a high-tension wire. Every day my lay-backs get a little deeper, and my body is moving in new ways, as if it's barely holding back something I didn't know I had. One night, Mom asks me if I've taken out the trash and I say *"Sí"* without thinking. In the moment before she frowns, shock blanks out her face, and I feel a sizzling pleasure.

Because Tony and Maria are using the stage, we're practicing in the cafeteria—"Neutral territory," Mr. Bixby says. By the silverware bins, I tap my foot and watch the "America" rehearsal stop because of Marina Rowe, who must have been cast as Rosalia because of her boobs, not that Mr. Bixby cares about them. She's a terrible dancer and can't remember any of her sixteen lines. But she's the only girl other than Maria who argues with haughty Anita, and even though Rosalia loses, it's still thrilling to watch someone take Anita on. Or it would be thrilling, if the person weren't Marina.

"What do you think you're arguing about?" Mr. Bixby says to her.

"Whether America is good or not."

"Deeper than that."

"Immigrants should go home?"

Mr. Bixby takes a deep breath, the one that signals we've just hit the end of his patience. "Inclusion. You're arguing to prove you belong. There's nothing more important than that."

"Okay," says Marina, happy to have the question answered for her.

"So how do you pour the hunger to be included into your dancing?"

"We ripple," she says promptly, then glances at his face. "We explode?"

Quietly, my feet moving lightly over the tile floor, I start again with the shuddering little steps, then the explosive kicks that make me cry out. I may be a sixteen-year-old German-Irish girl living in flat Ohio, but *West Side Story* is a chute I slide down, and every day I'm a little more Marisol, working in a West Side dress shop and kissing Pepe on the fire escape. When Jeff O'Brien, who plays Snowboy, bumped into me in the cafeteria, I hissed at him.

Mr. Bixby notices me marking out the steps, and I see him pause. I feel the moment like a hitch in the breath, and for a second all the sound in the cafeteria stops. He's never seen me before—or rather, he's never seen Marisol, sixteen years old and hungry for an American car, an American house and boy and life. She did not come here to mark out tiny steps in a white cinderblock room that smells like gravy. Can Mr. Bixby see my sneer? Mr. Bixby would be lucky to have Marisol walk over him in her sharp-pointed shoes. Promises have been made on every side, but so far all Marisol has been given is a script, the boys she has known all her life, and one small hope in being picked out by a man in tight pants and dancing shoes. I kick again, laying back into the air, which catches me.

Mr. Bixby claps his hands and sound rushes back in. "Again," he says. "Marisol, show them."

I swish my skirt, walking to the front of the room, and feel every set of eyes. We are living this play, almost all of us, and I wish a Jet were here so I could spit on him. This is my country now.

Comfort (1)

"Just tell the truth," they say, and I can't even count how many things are wrong with that sentence. There are a lot of truths, and most of them aren't on speaking terms with the others.

True: I am the man who killed a child. My family and friends don't believe that, pointing out that all my life I have liked kids. Also true, and irrelevant. People bring up stuff that they want to matter.

"Sam and Mark love you. They still talk about the kite you made them. We'll fight this," my sister says. She thinks there's a solution, but for there to be a solution, there has to be a problem.

I had never held a gun before. That thing people say about how a gun is surprisingly heavy? That's true. I fiddled with the trigger, then lifted the gun two-handed, like cops on TV, sighted a little boy kicking dirt behind the dugout, and fired. I was as surprised as anybody when the bullet went off. It turns out I'm a good shot.

The boy's mother says I am a monster. True. The prosecutor says that I have no concept of the value of human life. Not true. The value of that boy's life is my life, to the penny.

"It was an *accident!*" my sister wails. Why should that make any difference?

Before this happened I was a flight attendant. The point of the job is not to fulfill customers' needs, but to anticipate them—the blanket, the cargo space, the airsickness bag *fast.* "What if I'm the one getting airsick?" somebody asked in training school.

"You get airsick on your own time," the teacher said.

"So we put our needs last?"

"You're flight attendants. You don't have needs."

Other people groaned, but I smiled. For the first time in my life, I was right at home.

I know how to give mouth-to-mouth resuscitation. I can swim with a baby on my back. I can splint a broken leg and tie a tourniquet, and I know how to make three oxygen masks support five people. My job is to save lives, but no one at thirty thousand feet wants to think about battling for an oxygen mask, and so I hand out pretzels and squat in the aisle, grinning at the toddler furious to find herself imprisoned on a slightly grubby airplane seat. I used to do these things, before my airline let me go. "I'm sure you understand," the supervisor said, and he was right.

I had never done anything to hurt anyone, not even when my first boyfriend stabbed the upholstery of my car with a twelve-inch knife, or when another boyfriend gave me cocaine laced with laxative and then locked me in the bedroom. "I just wanted proof you were human," he said, and after I cleaned the room I let him stay for another five months because he had no place else to go and it didn't seem to make much difference, in the end. I was the guy who was too nice, until I murdered a little boy.

"Don't *say* it like that," my sister snaps.

"What did you think would happen when you squeezed the trigger?" the D.A. asks.

I was at my nephew's baseball game, wandering behind the bleachers during an endless inning, foul after foul after foul. The afternoon had turned spongy with boredom and humidity, and I felt trapped inside a dream of a life parallel to mine, one that circled around baseball games and coolers and a single half-full bottle of rye at home, in the cabinet above the refrigerator. Off by himself, one of the dads motioned to me, and I went to him. That's my training. When somebody calls, you go. "Check this out," he said, pulling a pistol from his jacket pocket. Gray, with lighter gray around the casing. "Glock 17. Gen4," he said.

"At a Little League game?"

"Nobody needs to know."

His eyes were bright as he raised and lowered the

gun—not sighting through it, just hefting it, excited with the feel in his hand. I knew before he asked that he was going to let me touch it.

"Did you know that the gun was loaded?" Everybody asks, but the question never occurred to me. When you pick up a gun in a dream, you don't ask if it's loaded.

"You didn't *know!*" my sister says. The ordeal has been hard on her. Her pretty face has gone muddy and she hasn't gotten her hair done in weeks. I see her husband looking at the seam of gray at her hairline. "No one can blame you for what you didn't know," she says, her voice shrill with repetition.

That's the stupidest thing she's said yet. What kind of idiot pulls a trigger and expects nothing to happen? My old boyfriend texted me that I had set back the cause of gay rights ten years, because even a decent homo would know how to handle a gun. The man at the game, the gun's owner, said, "The action on it is smooth. Hardly no kick." I don't mean that he was encouraging me to find out. That was my own idea.

I was supposed to fly to Chicago that night. My suitcase was already packed. I knew where I would stay for the night, and how early I'd have to get up for the flight back the next day. I knew how many bottles were supposed to be on the airline bar cart, and how many I could palm to help me get to sleep. I knew a number I could call if I didn't want to be alone. I knew that man beside me under the bleachers would have shoved me to the ground if I had reached out to touch his chest, at the same time that he was putting a goddamn gun in my hands.

After I shot the boy, a moment passed before I heard the screams and felt the gun ripped away. The day's spongy haziness vanished into stark, dazzling light, and in the shining split second when nothing had yet changed, I looked at my sister, her face brilliant. She shook her head again and again: No, no, no, no, no. Then the next part started.

Comfort (2)

Nothing to prepare you. Nothing to say. "We're here for you," my friends repeat, and I hear the anguish in their voices. They mean the best, they mean love, but, Jesus, they need to go away. "You can't be alone now," my mother says, and then amends it to "You shouldn't be alone," which is righter, but there's only one person I want to be with, and he's gone.

I did everything exactly right, every step by the book. Bobby had no idea what even my tits looked like until our wedding night, something we made tense jokes about later. At least they got big when I was pregnant; he liked that. I quit my job and painted the nursery a sweet green, a color that would welcome the five children I planned on. Bobby was doing well at the dealership, meeting his quotas and getting his bonuses. I saw life stretching out like a wide, pretty pasture without so much as a stone to get in my shoe. That's how you think when you're young.

After Jason was toddling, I saw Bobby's mouth tighten when I talked about the next one. I went to Victoria's Secret and bought a teddy that the salesgirl said was perfect for little girls like me. "The ruffles are your friends. They give the look of fullness right where it counts." Shyly, I pulled it on that night after we put Jason down, and Bobby blushed. He kissed my forehead and left the room.

When he moved in with his massively titted girlfriend, he was good to me. He made sure that his child-support payments came in time to cover the mortgage, and when I had trouble finding a job at first he asked his friends to look out for me. He had a lot of friends.

"He's a decent man," I said.

"You need so much more," Mama said.

I gestured at my boy, who was frowning at the pyramid of Legos he had built, trying to see where he could fit his toy truck. "I've got riches."

Mama's face softened, but she still said, "No, you don't."

When Jason turned four, he vandalized our neighbor's iris bed to bring me a bouquet. At six, he brought me breakfast in bed: a microwaved cheese sandwich. He wouldn't go to sleep unless I came into his room, smoothed his hair, and told him I loved him. When his teacher told him to draw a picture of the person he liked best in the world, he drew a figure with long red fingernails and a pennant of yellow hair, with my name in his brand-new printing. "I don't look anything like that," I said, and he said, "That's what you really look like, underneath."

My son was the only male I knew who looked at me. Every day men came into the bank and didn't ever notice the flat-chested gal counting out twenties. "Don't you meet anyone at that place?" Mama said, and I told her no. Easier than telling her that I met people every day, over and over. Exactly once did a man ask my name. He said, "Claudette. That's pretty." A month or so later he came back needing a cashier's check for $300, and asked my name. "Claudette. That's pretty."

Named after my dad. I saved some boy from being Claude Jr.

Jason thought that Claude was the funniest name in the world, so I threatened him with it all the time. "I'm your mother! I gave you your name; I can change it!" "Just don't name me CLOD," he would yell, delighted.

He used to yell. We used to collapse in laughter at the kitchen table, one or the other whispering "Clod" to set us off again. We did that before Jason was shot to death at a baseball game by a gay man holding a gun for the first time in his life.

"He didn't even know him!" people said. What difference would that have made? Dead is dead, a sentence people don't want to hear. Some others: God doesn't have a plan; Jason is in a box, not a better place; Thank you for coming, please leave. I didn't mean to be ugly, but there are no words that help, and twice I wound up having to comfort a visitor who couldn't bear my tragedy. "God doesn't give us more than we can handle," my mother's friend said. I scrounged up a thin smile for her and said, "I'm still standing."

"God has a plan."

I sent her home with a slice of pound cake that someone else had brought.

And then I closed the house. I called Mama once a day to let her know I was breathing, but otherwise I didn't open the blinds or answer the door. I had enough food in the refrigerator to see me through a month, and I ate the bits that I liked, mostly the brownie edges, and let the rest spoil. I listened to the silence, training myself not to listen for my boy. Day after day I laid down on the grief and rolled on it as if I were rolling on broken glass, trying to get all the hurt over at once. It took me a while to learn that glass keeps cutting; that's its nature, like it's skin's nature to flinch from the cut. The cutting never stops, or the hurting. The night after I figured that out I raised the blinds and went out for Diet Coke, the first thing I'd run through.

I attended every minute of the trial, conducted not so that we could discover who killed Jason—two bored girls had been talking behind the bleachers and saw everything—but so the jury could decide on a sentence. The killer was a pleasant-looking guy with sandy hair and tended hands. "His eyes look dead," Mama said, but I didn't see that. To me he looked nice.

During the trial, through the days of testimony, he cried. Mama was enraged. "How about crying before you pull the trigger, gay boy?" she railed once we got home. "How dare you come in here now and act sorry?"

"Maybe he is," I said.

"Don't you even start," she snarled. For three solid weeks, the length of the trial and deliberation, she didn't say a civil word to anybody. Then the killer—Jeffrey, I knew his name by now—got life, no parole, and Mama fell against me and screamed like an animal.

A second round of brownies and visitors has started since then, people eager to share my pain. The church choir director says, "I can at least sleep now, knowing that he's locked up. Even though jail's too good for him." She leans forward. "He's probably getting just what he wants in there."

"Maybe he is."

"At least you saw justice served. At least he's locked up. Now you can get on with your life."

"My life has nothing to do with him."

The ones who are paying attention get careful then, and start asking if I'm taking care of myself and maybe need to see a doctor. There's no shame in a little Xanax these days.

I haven't become one of those forgive-everybody types. I would cheerfully send Jeffrey to the electric chair if I could back-wind the clock and reclaim my boy. But watching my friends and neighbors drip poison while they talk about Jeffrey leaves me feeling worse, and I've started taking walks in the late afternoon, when people tend to come by. I closed my Facebook account, and I wipe out a lot of emails.

I'm used to a house now that is so still I could hear a ghost's footstep, if only it would come. Mama would be alarmed if she heard me talking about ghosts; she's already afraid that I've imperiled my immortal soul by saying "goddamn" when the minister visited. She doesn't like to admit that a life can happen with no instruction manual, and that's where I dwell now. I live in a universe that is boundless and godless and contains only me. It's not as terrible as you might think. The worst thing that can possibly happen has happened, and now I am safe.

I think that if I told that to Jeffrey, he would understand. Not that I'll do it. It's just the kind of idea that keeps me going late at night in my quiet house.

Compliments

FOR J.G.

"I like your accent."

"You have nice eyes."

"You seem really smart."

No, she doesn't. She seems dumb as a rock, and I'm just about ready to say so. We freshmen have had group-building exercises all morning, with pizza vouchers going to the person who memorizes the most names or correctly links the right person with the right hometown. Now we are responsible for giving compliments to every single person in our fifteen-person group. We're lined up, as if ready to meet a firing squad. The girl next to me wears sparkly barrettes. *Turn-ons include kittens and hot cocoa in front of a blazing fire.*

The complimenting girl has almost made it down the line to me. She started strong, but she's losing steam.

"You have cool shoes." Then, "I like your backpack." And now, face-to-face, girl-to-girl: "I'll bet you get a lot of good grades."

The next complimenter has already started, overlapping the first one. The people running this thing, probably sociology students itching to put their new skills to work, didn't plan out their time very well, and we've only got ten minutes for 225 compliments. You'd think upper classmen would have done the arithmetic. The compliments take longer now, because we're not supposed to repeat and the easy ones are disappearing fast.

"Your voice is nice."

"That's a cool bracelet."

"I saw you running this morning. You went really fast."

The complimenter is supposed to hold the gaze of the complimentee. How can the sociology majors think that this will build group spirit? If I see any of these people six months from now, I'll remember the long gaze and the lies, and I'll hide.

"Your shirt's a nice color," the complimenter says to sparkly barrettes. *Turn-ons include kittens and hot anal sex in front of a blazing fire.*

"Your smile looks like you're keeping secrets," the complimenter tells me, and one of the sociology majors says, "That's not a compliment."

"Yes, it is," I say.

The two who are finished take their place at the end

of the line—they've done the hard part, but they still have to be complimented. They're whispering and looking over at the corner where the sociology majors made us put our phones in a box. The compliments, more and more stiff, tip over like dominos, all coercion and no truth, like conversation over Christmas dinner. "You have nice earrings." "I like your shirt."

"You can go beyond appearances," one of the sociology majors calls out.

"I'll bet you're a nice person," the complimenter promptly says, and I have to give it to him for quickness. To sparkly barrettes he says, "I'll bet you're gentle around old people."

Turn-ons include kittens and hot anal sex in front of a blazing house fire.

To me he says, "I'll bet you're not gentle around old people," and the sociology majors make him do it again, even though I feel totally complimented. "I'll bet you have good music." He gazes at me, just like he's supposed to.

"Shit," says one of the others. "That's a good one."

No, it isn't. All morning I've stayed well under the radar, not just of the sociology majors, but of my new classmates. This is my skill: I can disappear in plain sight. If a picture is taken of us, something that seems dismally likely, it will seem as if there are fourteen people in the group, none of them me. Now I've got my co-freshmen assessing me, and I need to be careful. I do have a lot of good music.

We're over our ten minutes, and everybody's getting restless. The sociology majors have had to swat one of the guys away from the box with the phones. We're all hungry, and there's a smell of tomato sauce from the cafeteria next door.

"You have good color sense."

"Nice job with your hair."

"I can tell you like green."

What qualifies as a compliment, anyway? A mere fact shouldn't count. The longer this goes on, the more sharply I see every one of us, sunburned knees and makeup lines and one guy with really nice hands, and for the love of Christ it's sparkly barrettes' turn to compliment. She giggles.

"Are you a design major? Because the way you put those bracelets together totally rocks."

"Are you an engineering major? Lucky you. You're actually going to be employed."

This is like Guess Your Astrological Sign: College Edition. I can't blame her for finding an angle and working it. I'm just surprised she was able to do it.

She's good at maintaining the eye contact, too. "Are you a psych major?" she says to me.

"I'm not any major yet. I haven't even had a class."

"You look like you know things," she says, her eyes boring into mine. *Turn-ons include kitten-eating snakes and house fires.*

"I know I wish this exercise was over."

"Well, yeah." She moves to the dude next to me, leaving the rest of her comment unsaid: *Do you think you're special?*

Kittens chopped up by chain saws. Anal rape. Conflagration.

Now it's my turn, and there are no compliments left in the world. People's eyes are red from so much staring, and I have never felt so visible in my life. Everybody wants me to hurry up already; it smells like lasagna next door. But I can't think of a damn thing to say. The girl before me cracks a little smile. "Hurry up," she says.

"You're very punctual," I say, kissing good-bye to any hope of ever making friends.

Next: "You don't feel the need to be too neat."

"You know what's in fashion."

"I'll bet you have a dog."

Eventually it's sparkly barrettes. I say, "You would have found room on a life boat from the *Titanic.*"

"I love that movie!" She leans forward and squeezes my hand. "Do you really think so?"

"Totally."

Her face is an astonishment. It might actually be emitting light. "Best. Compliment. Ever."

Gently, I try to get my hand back. "That's great. Really."

"I didn't think you'd be good at this, but you're the best one here."

"See what a good compliment can do?" says one of the sociology majors.

"Is anybody else hungry?" says the dude next to me.

I pry my hand back and finish up the line with rerun compliments; everybody's sick of the exercise now, and we're all starving. But sparkly barrettes is bearing down on me before we leave the room. "I missed your name at the beginning," she says.

"Eileen."

She smiles. "Hey, Eileen. When the ship starts to go? I'm taking you with me."

The Tenth Student

One out of ten. The other nine slump into my house because their parents send them, and they lie about practicing. When I put the sheet music up, they squint at it, unsure where to put their hands on the keyboard. "I'm so busy! I'm not like you. I have a lot of things to do."

No one else's life is ever real, is it? Especially the life that belongs to the wispy-haired piano teacher with the bad apartment and the good Baldwin. That life is a soap bubble until the tenth student comes in, the fifteen-year-old with the long hands that are constantly moving. "There has to be a way to make a crescendo at the da capo," the tenth student says. "Isn't that what I want?"

Stupid people imagine that the living dream of music is happy. They've never looked at the tenth student's trembling mouth, just on the brink of an expression. Exultation is exhausting.

The tenth student isn't here to learn how to play. The tenth student knows everything about playing. I teach the tenth student what the music can bring: our ruination. The music wants to bore into the heart of the universe, find the black, hot, embracing core, and bring it back for the rest of us. The music wants to expand our souls until they shatter. This is the reason I've torn my nails to shreds by the time the tenth student comes for the weekly lesson, even though the tenth student arrives early, a personality trait. The tenth student comes early, pays up, and when the tenth student plays I brace myself and then still flinch, because the fulfillment of beauty is always shocking.

My tax return lists me as a music teacher, but the truth is that I listen for my living. I've heard everything whispered outside my apartment—the jokes, the gasps, the shushed repetitions. Language is as flipper-footed as a seal, and it allows us only to say a few blunt things over and over, so I have learned not to say *love* or *beauty* or *special*. I barely say *talent*. One student was taken away from me just as the student began to approach rapture, a word I was idiot enough to use. The world is poorer now, and the student is in Florida, enrolled in a college program that teaches hospitality.

I don't claim to be the only one who can listen. Often

the parents of students one through nine make a point of coming to the lessons and listening to every word I say, glaring. "Help yourself to coffee or water," I say; "the bathroom's right down there."

"I'm fine," says the glowering parent, not about to leave a defenseless child with a teacher who talks about rapture.

Students one through nine mostly hear what they're told to hear, though every once in a while, when the seasons are changing and the air tilts, they sometimes hear the edge of something new. They change their posture and shift unhappily on the piano bench; who ever said that we want to hear a thing we never heard before? "That," I say. "Play that." They don't; they're one through nine. Usually they stop playing well before they come close to the sharp moment, quick as a pin, that stops their breath. I'm the one who hears it.

After they leave, one through ten, I play, and cats run away. Students scuffle outside my house, standing at the window and straining to hear. I don't care when one through nine are there; they think I sound perfect, which is depressing, or that I sound just like them, which is also depressing and closer to true. I play so the tenth student can hear me.

The music I make is bricks tumbling down metal staircases, a fork tine screed over glass. It is a screen door slammed eight times in a row. It is a concrete block heaved over the edge of a rowboat, slamming a still-breathing body to the bottom of a lake. It is the entire sparkling universe snapped in two, like an LP over the knee of a piano teacher.

I play every night.

Second Sight

Liz's mother, Hannah, knew Liz and I were going to Ocracoke for our anniversary before I did. Hannah believes she has psychic powers, though I'm never sure what she intuits and what Liz breaks down and tells her. Hannah doesn't like being left out of things, and if she discerns a secret, there's hell to pay. She told me brightly, "Ocracoke is nice this time of year. Not so crowded."

"How did you know we were thinking about Ocracoke?"

"I know what Liz is thinking. So I asked, and she told me."

Liz and I were in a rough patch, and neither one of us had felt like talking about an anniversary celebration. I'd been looking at some Ocracoke websites, that's all. Maybe Liz saw them on our computer and told her mom. Maybe.

We went, and it wasn't crowded. The whole time

we were there, I thought about Hannah and wondered whether she knew what her daughter and I were doing—mostly, not talking to each other and drinking maybe just a little bit too much Chardonnay. When I said, "Where are you? You're a million miles away," Liz said, "I'm right here. Right where I want to be." Then we sat another half hour without a word.

After we got home, Liz washed her own clothes and left my unwashed laundry in a meticulous pile at the end of the bed, where it still sits. I can't even tell you what we're fighting about, though I'm desperate to fix it.

We met—where else?—at a gay bar in Columbus, like half of our friends. I found out that she was funny and smart and owned her own house. She noticed when a woman near us stopped drinking, and quietly told the bartender to keep serving her; Liz would pay the bill. *Observant*, I thought. *Kind*. It didn't occur to me to ask whether she lived next to a narcissistic, touchy, arguably psychic mother who had a love life more complicated than the national budget. We learn the lessons we need to know too late.

Some crisis is always at the boil in Hannah's life, the new woman she loves or man she hates, and Liz and I allot one solid day a week to Hannah management. Today, because I can't think of anybody else to ask, I've invited Hannah to come over. I feel like I'm edging onto a minefield, though all I'm doing is making my mother-in-law some tea.

At the kitchen table, she shakes her hair back from her unnervingly green eyes. Liz told me that Hannah got contacts lenses to enhance the glow.

"How are you and Lizzie doing? I haven't seen you lately."

It's been four days since she was here for dinner. "Rough."

The mug between Hannah's hands is chipped. Liz and I need to get some decent mugs. "Liz isn't happy, and I don't know if I'm the problem or not. She won't tell me." I swallow. "I'm afraid it's somebody else."

"Has she said anything?"

In the last three days Liz has said about eight words, four of them about the filthy tub. "What do you think?"

Hannah wouldn't pause so long if she didn't know something. "You're a thoughtful person. It was kind to make tea for me."

"Good grief, Hannah. It's just a cup of tea." I'm thinking I should offer her some cookies, but the look on Hannah's face changes, and suddenly I'm aware of the planes of her face and how close her hand is to mine on the table. If she's psychic, she should be able to feel my stomach plummet. "Cookies?" I blurt, moving my hand away.

She lets a moment pass. "I have an appointment coming up. I need to get ready," she says, though she doesn't move.

When I try to speak again, my voice has deserted me. I croak, "I would do anything for Liz."

"Don't tell her that. She doesn't like to feel crowded."

Hannah's face is suddenly severe, a line of afternoon shadow cutting down her cheek. "Give her some room. She'll come back to you." Not hard to imagine the turban and the crystal ball.

When Hannah hugs me good-bye, I pretend not to feel how hard she pulls me in. Later I'll see her makeup mark on the shoulder of my sweater.

I leave the house before Liz comes home and text her that I'll be home late. She's reading in the living room when I come home after eight o'clock, and greets me with the first smile I've seen in a while.

In the days that follow I keep my distance, and at night she runs her fingernails through my hair, along my scalp, until I shiver. We go to dinner at Hannah's; she nods as she watches Liz and me, and rubs my knee under the table. I volunteer to wash the dishes while Hannah and Liz are watching a murder on ID: Discovery. Hannah's a messy cook and her saucepans are horrifying, but it's soothing to scrub away for a few minutes, until Hannah comes in.

"Who killed the guy?"

"Commercial. You can just let that soak."

"I don't mind scrubbing. It's stress relief."

"Are you stressed?"

Well, I am now, feeling her breath on my neck. "Things are going better between Liz and me."

"I could tell. You two are laughing now. I love it when you laugh."

There's a baked-on bit of something on the saucepan,

big as a freckle. I put my whole weight into getting it off, and Hannah runs her finger down my arm. "I should sic you on all of my pots."

When I turn around, Hannah's so close that I'm already in her arms, already crying. "What kind of marriage is this? She only likes me when I'm far away."

"Shh," Hannah says, kissing my neck. She doesn't seem to mind how I stiffen. "She loves you. She just doesn't like to be bored."

I'm doing the awful kind of crying, snot everywhere. Stretching to keep my mouth away from hers, I say, "Is marriage boring?" From the living room, gunfire.

Hannah reaches to push a curl out of my eye. Liz's voice from the doorway is exasperated. "Christ, Mom, what do you think you're doing?"

"Saving your marriage."

"Doesn't look like it."

"Do you want to grab her and go home?"

"Yes."

"You're welcome."

The laugh that flares between them is explosive, and far away from my sudden, soggy anger. Still laughing, Liz takes one of my hands. "Come into the living room. They're about to arraign the guy who stole the gun." In that moment, her eyes flashing, she looks exactly like her mother. This is what she will look like in twenty-five years.

Hannah looks at me triumphantly. "Let the pot soak. It will clean itself."

She's wrong. I leave them and scrub it for another ten minutes after the show is over. The sound of their laughter in the living room is familiar and steady and I don't want to hear it anymore, like a song I've played all the pleasure out of.

Phantom

I can hear the music from the driveway—the awful see-saw of the voice, the gluey strings, the whole melodramatic marshmallow mess of it. *Phantom of the Opera*. My wife, Sarah, must be going out of her mind.

This has to be Carmina's doing, which means it's well intended, though I don't know how much intentions matter right now. Sarah's got maybe seventy-two hours left, and she doesn't want to spend any of them listening to Andrew Lloyd Webber.

Disarmingly cute, Carmina greets me at the front door to take the grocery bags. Like so many hospice workers, she's Filipina, five feet tall with hair disciplined into a bun, and dimples punctuating her round cheeks. When she says she loves her work, I believe her. She puts her ear right to Sarah's silently moving mouth, then translates for us. "She wants juice," or "She's cold. I'm going to give her another blanket." Now Sarah gets whatever she wants. Why hasn't that been true all her life? I don't have an answer.

When Sarah is sleeping, Carmina asks us about her. Did she go to church? Does she have a favorite movie? No, no. After a while I start to feel embarrassed, as if Sarah should have more going for her. "She played the French horn," I offer, and Carmina nods.

"She played in the symphony," Sarah's sister Margaret says, irritated with me for not giving Sarah her proper respect. This is the siblings' take on me—that I condescend to Sarah, that I always condescended to her. They're not about to listen to me tell them they don't know their own sister, how she'd stroll around the kitchen with her thumbs looped into invisible suspenders, informing the universe that she was a *professional musician*, back when she could still walk.

"That's right," I say. "Symphony."

Carmina nods again, and says, "Classical?"

"Wagner," Margaret says. Margaret is a massive snob and Sarah can't stand her, but we don't get to pick who stands next to our deathbed. Someone needs to fix that.

"Wagner," Carmina says carefully.

Maybe "Wagner" sounds like "Webber" to her. Maybe she just remembers a two-syllable name. Or maybe she likes *Phantom of the Opera*, thinks it sounds like classical music, and that's why "Music of the Night" is pouring out of the living room where we've set up Sarah's hospital bed, too big to fit in the bedroom. I used to tease her by humming this song until she said that she wanted to pull her ears off.

"Maybe we should turn this down?" I say to Carmina.

"Maybe we should turn it *off*," Margaret says when I get to the kitchen.

"You don't have to stay."

"I'm on my way out. Promise you'll turn this off the second you can."

"Scout's honor." If Margaret thought for one moment, she'd know I was never a Scout, but one of the things I can count on about Margaret is that she won't think.

Carmina leaves at six, relieved by one of a rotating staff of night nurses. When the first one appeared with her knitting and doctor's bag, I asked if I couldn't take care of the night duties, mostly watching over Sarah's sleep. It seemed a good task for a husband. Carmina rested her gentle hand on mine. "She needs medicine." Later the siblings told me she meant morphine, and I felt stupid. I don't know why they all knew.

I lunge for the volume as soon as Carmina's car is gone. Sarah doesn't register any change, barely making a ripple under the sheet, 105 pounds of compromised breathing and faltering heart. She's fifty-two, and her cancer is everywhere—liver, colon, most recently lungs. I imagine little blobs of cancer racing around her body and giggling as they create new outposts, another inelegant thought Margaret would chide me for. The night nurse looks at me curiously but doesn't ask anything. I'm not sure she speaks English. Now the room is all but silent, and I can hear Sarah's torn breathing. She hasn't been able to play her French horn for nearly a year. I miss the full sound, the pretty *hey, tally-ho!* of it, and go to the stereo to change out *Phantom* for Strauss's horn concerto, as pretty as it gets.

Immediately Sarah stirs, her forehead lightly creased. Carmina told us to expect to see changes as Sarah reached the end—her mouth might move, or she might pluck at the sheet. "These are autonomic responses. Her body is shutting down," Carmina said, and I've been waiting ever since for a shutting-down sound I imagine like a car door closing.

I sit close to her and take her hand, but she pulls away, something else Carmina told us to expect. "Her arms and legs will contract. She may not know you are here. The medicine shuts her off to the world." Because I am a monster, I wish I could take away her medicine. I want her to know that I'm here.

With a snap, the night nurse turns off the music, and Sarah relaxes into her pillow as if the nurse had turned her off, too. So no Strauss. The oxygen tank that Sarah hates hisses from the corner. We only use it when her breathing gets especially tortured, a distinction no one should have to make. Otherwise the room is still. The night nurse has gone back to the bedroom where she's watching TV. She keeps the sound off.

Everything in a death room makes noise. When I

shift on the bed, the metal frame softly clicks. The palm of my hand stroking Sarah's hair makes a shushing sound, as if I'm reproving myself. Powered by capable lungs and heart, I'm as ungainly and rude as a Shakespeare bumpkin. "Zounds, m'lady," I say softly, a joke she would have laughed at to humor me. When the mere sound of my breath starts to feel like a jackhammer, I reach for the book on the side table, cluttered with washcloths and empty plastic cups. Margaret must have left this book: *On Death and Dying*.

Sarah smiles when she hears my snicker, an expression that is not, *not*, an autonomic response. I gaze at her sunken eyes, the shadows around them bruise colored, and her lovely mouth, now chapped and flaking. Out of my mouth, unintentionally at first, comes "Music of the Night," my gooiest version yet. I don't let myself think that it might be our last joke, but the knowledge is in the room like another presence, more real than I am.

Sarah's face twists. She might be getting a leg cramp, or fearing it—phantom pain. Either way, her lips are moving, and like Carmina, I put my ear to her mouth where I can feel her mouth brushing the skin of my ear. I can't make out any words, and so choose what she might be saying.

I hum all night, and in the morning let Carmina discover for herself that she's gone.

Cloth

It is nothing short of a miracle that the zipper closes. Patsy's wearing one girdle on top of another one, so she won't be able to sit down or breathe all night, but she'll look stacked in this number that's tight up at the boobs and then spangles all down below. "Gown," she calls it. It's a dress, and it's too tight, and she looked better five years ago in fringe and cowboy boots.

Five years ago she didn't need a dresser, though, so I should count my blessings. She's saying she wants a driver, too, which is a good idea. The way she takes corners, that wagon isn't going to last to the end of the year. "I ride my cars like I ride Charlie!" she half yells. Nobody ever has to ask if Patsy's in the house.

We hurry to get her onstage on time. She didn't arrive with a second to spare, and then had to talk to every single fan on her way in. She's famous for talking to folks, even when I tell her she didn't work since she was twelve to hear Norma, visiting from Oklahoma City, tell her how much powdered sugar she puts in her sand tarts. "These people give me a job," she says, and that's right of course.

She doesn't show good sense, is the thing. She can't tell what's good from trash. When she first heard "Walkin' After Midnight," she hated it. Had to be dragged to record it. Same with "I Fall to Pieces." Same with "Crazy." What did she want to record? *Yodeling.* Like the Winchester, Virginia, hayseed she still is. "I'm country, is what I am, and they keep trying to make me sing these little pop songs." Listen to yourself, Patsy Cline. If you're country, what are you doing squeezing yourself into a $300 gown? Nashville is full of people who are fooling themselves, and Patsy's at the front of the parade.

A roar of happy laughter. She's just said something mildly risqué, the kind of joke that will please the audience, who think she's letting them in on something special. Patsy would never dare tell them the kinds of jokes she tells me every day. The *mouth* on that gal. She is rough as a cob, and everybody backstage knows it. Once every couple of months she comes in with pancake makeup not covering what Charlie did to her the night before. Maybe that's why she takes those long road trips with Bill, her manager. Men can't stay away from Patsy, and Patsy can't stay away from men. "Hoss"—she calls everybody "Hoss," male, female, and God—"the good Lord gave me eyes to appreciate a fine-looking man, and the snatch to give him a ride. He wouldn't want me to ignore His blessings, would he?" And then the laugh. It's hard not to have a good time around Patsy. I just worry about her.

This town's so full of sponges, I'm surprised the sidewalks don't make a sucking noise when you walk. People come here with empty pockets and bellies, and every one of them finds Patsy. Once I saw her promise to give her bed—her *bed*—to some hobo she'd met ten minutes before. She caught my look and said, "Hoss, I can buy a bed before tonight. He can't." It's as close as she comes to an apology.

She doesn't always have my salary on hand. When she hired me, I made sure we had a written contract between us that set out my paydays. Even still, some months it comes the first and she says, "Hoss, let me take you out to dinner. You'll have to wait a little for your pay, but I can make sure you eat." She looks pained, and it's all I can do not to say, "Patsy, honey, it is a pleasure and a privilege to stuff you into your tight gowns. Don't you worry about that ol' salary." My landlady has told me that the next time my rent is late, I'll find somebody else staying in my room.

I'm not special. Lots of people here are living on fumes, waiting for success to stop for them. Nothing shameful in that. But it's when Patsy slings her arm around me and says, "Hoss, we understand, don't we? We're cut out of the same cloth," that I start to feel my dander come up. Does she think that I stand before my closet every morning and ponder which pretty, full-skirted dress I'm going to wear? Which bright red lipstick? Does she think I wait till everybody leaves on the first of the month and then hold out my hand to her because it's fun? And what does she see, looking at my life with no car and no house, that she thinks she wants?

Once she called me to come over to her house and keep her company. Charlie was out someplace and she hated to be alone. I drank coffee, she drank coffee with whiskey, and we talked men and music and men. "I don't trust Charlie," she said, her breath velveted with Jim Beam. "I love him, but I don't trust him." Unfolding her legs, she went over to the fireplace, wiggled loose a brick, and pulled out an envelope. "Look here. This is one thousand dollars. Charlie don't know it's here. I keep it because you never know."

"Don't tell me this, Patsy."

"I have to tell somebody."

I stood up. "Not me."

Her eyes filled. People who hear her talk underestimate how tender she is. That's how she makes us cry when she sings. "Okay, Hoss, you never saw it."

"Good." We weren't friends. She was my boss.

She pays me $200 a month. Often she finds a reason to give me more—because I hemmed a dress or cleaned her makeup mirror or swept the perpetually gritty cement floor of the dressing room. I look for those tasks, and don't let myself think about the last time Patsy swept her own floor. Humming "Walkin' After Midnight" helps. You can tap your toe to it and her voice is smooth as honey.

Once she told me she wanted to do some grocery shopping, and would I come with her? Patsy did her own shopping, but she didn't usually ask for company. Still, I met her at the Bi-Lo. Pretty yellow dress and enough lipstick to kiss her way through the Seventh Battalion. The second people saw her, there was a commotion, and she pulled me to her and grinned. A pop of a flashbulb. I was a rube not to see this coming.

The store manager came out, all smiles. "Miss Patsy Cline! I guess even Nashville stars need to buy groceries." Pop. Pop.

"You bet they do, Hoss."

"You don't have servants to buy your groceries for you?"

"No sir, just my friend here. I need"—she fished up a piece of paper from her handbag—"two cans of tomatoes and a good chuck roast. I'll make dinner tonight and Charlie won't know what hit him!" Everybody laughed and Patsy winked, linked arms with me, and toured the store. Then she left, and the manager lifted his eyebrows. It was up to me to put away the cans she'd gotten out of order.

When I got home that afternoon there was a big stain on my blouse, where it would show in the photos. Soaked right into the fibers. Not ever coming out. That night at the Ryman, the audience wouldn't stop yelling until Patsy sang "I Fall to Pieces" a second time, when you could hear the cry in her voice.

Right then, I figured, Patsy was at home with Charlie, wearing the peignoir that drives him wild. I don't have a peignoir; I have a nightgown. It's cotton that's perfectly fine until a person finds out about satin. That's what talent does to you—it teaches you what other people don't even think about. And then you're never like other people again. Even if you want to be, even if you try. Even Little Jimmy Dickens, with all his Tater talk, will cut you short and walk away like he's never seen you if it's getting on to show time. Because he can. Because he has to. Patsy will be doing it soon. She'll give me $1,000 like it's nothing, because to her it won't be, and I'll look her in the eye and ask for more.

Friendship

—Was Nick the one with red hair?

—That was Garth the Goth. Total poseur. He had pentagram tattoos on his leg and baseball posters on his bedroom walls.

—He brought you to his house?

—Even poseur Goth boys have to live somewhere. And he was an okay kisser.

—As good as Hot Hank?

—I wish you didn't have such a good memory.

—He was the only one you bragged about.

—Not true. I distinctly remember bragging about Antoine.

—I will not listen to anything related to your year abroad.

—My French wasn't good enough to keep up with

him, so God only knows what he was saying in bed. Maybe the periodic table—he was a chemistry major. Seemed to excite him, at least.

—The men we know do not prize imagination. Knew.

—Know. You're married, not dead.

—It changes things. If I want to remember Republican Jeff, I have to go off for dinner with you and a bottle of wine so we can relive our old bad choices.

—You must have had worse choices than Republican Jeff.

—There was Jens. He owned a lot of T-shirts.

—You never told me about him. What did he have, leprosy?

—Three kids and a wife.

—I wouldn't have judged you.

—I judged myself. All that time you and I spent in the Women's Studies lobby, saying we weren't responsible for somebody else's vows? Turns out we are.

—So you broke things off?

—His wife did. She was waiting at my bus stop when I got off work and told me that once every few months she cleaned up after Jens, getting rid of his trash.

—So much for sisterhood.

—What was she supposed to do, hug me? I need more wine.

—We both need more wine. Or don't.

—Definitely do. We haven't even gotten to Frank. Great cocaine, awful breath. How could you stand to kiss him?

—My nose was so wrecked from his coke that I mostly didn't smell his breath. I didn't let myself think about his teeth.

—How was he in bed?

—Active. Does your husband know that you're asking about other men's sexual prowess?

—No. Active-good or active-bad?

—Active-coked-up. Are things okay?

—I am plying my friend with wine to get her to tell me details about her old boyfriends. What do you think?

—There doesn't have to be anything wrong with that.

—Thus speaks Unmarried.

—Men know wife material when they see it.

—And that's what I am?

—Don't sound miffed. You're someone's one and only.

—I can be miffed if I want. Women friends are supposed to support each other.

—Thus speaks Married. What would you do if you weren't?

—I'd get my married friends to tell me about their sex lives, because I couldn't imagine night after night after night after night with the same man. And some afternoons.

—As bad as that?

—At some point since the bouquet and the cake, a door closed. I didn't even hear it. Now I'm a wife.

—My door slides. I can see through it, but it's still closed.

—And there you stand, with your nose up to the glass? Don't ask me to pity you. You can open your door.

—Golly. Why didn't I think of that? Maybe I was just distracted, wishing I was married, like you. How wonderful it must be.

—Plenty of distraction to go around. Last night, while I was lying awake, I thought about you. You might have been watching TV. You might have had somebody's cock in your mouth. You might have been trimming your bangs.

—You better believe it. Three o'clock in the morning, with the cuticle scissors in front of the mirror and the taste of come in my mouth.

—Hélène Cixous made it sound better than that. I was lying in bed while my husband gently farted beside me.

—Do you think he dreams of other women?

—If he did, we wouldn't be having this conversation.

—People can surprise you.

—Not husbands.

—There was a party a long time ago. You two were barely married.

—What are you about to tell me?

—I was in the kitchen and he pinned me at the sink. He told me that he's not the kind of guy who has affairs, but if he were, he'd have one with me.

Say something.

—What were you wearing?

—Don't say that.

—He got me a blue top once that laced up the collar. He never notices clothes, but he told me he thought it would look pretty on me.

—I was probably wearing a T-shirt. I never had a top that laced.

—Maybe there was another party, and another woman in the kitchen.

—I'm not special?

—What did you tell him?

—You were my friend.

—Lucky me. I guess.

—Tell me what is the right reaction when your friend's husband assumes you're available, except for his high morals. What would Jens's wife have wanted you to say?

—Good-bye.

—Is that what you're saying?

—Is there more wine?

—Always.

—Then not yet.

Hallelujah Day

I've been back at the compound for five days and have already picked a fight with my mother. New land-speed record. I suggested that she take some local women to the village well to teach them how to avoid diarrhea in their babies. She got sidetracked into talking about baptism, and the next thing you know I had to shoulder her out of the way because she'd gotten into immersion versus sprinkling and was heading ninety to nothing toward baptismal regeneration. Three women had already drifted away, and we only started with seven.

Now I need to apologize to her. The diarrhea lesson was my idea, not hers. She's happier talking about heaven, which she's sure will have the golden sidewalks and the harps, and when I remind her that we still have to attend to our earthly lives, annoyance clouds her features. She is fervent, Lord love her. And the Lord probably does love her, which makes me both exasperated and grateful, since somebody's got to do it.

Along with a handful of other missionaries, Mom and I are spending a year volunteering for Christian Outreach, situated on a tiny island off of a tiny island off of a smallish island in the central Philippines. Not at all my kind of thing, but Mom caught me at a weak moment, when I'd broken up with my boyfriend and a holiday in the tropics sounded good. Mom came raring to talk faith, but the folks here don't want to talk about their everlasting souls. They want to talk about electricity and the possibility of another well on the island. Every Sunday we lustily lead prayer and song in the shanty church built by the group before us, and the locals sing gamely along, shooting me annoyed looks meant to remind me of Panasonic refrigerators that defrost themselves.

We aren't the only missionary group on Bacoyan Island, small enough to circumnavigate by foot in a day. On the east side, catching the good morning light, is Glory and Hosanna, a much noisier crowd who sing praise songs while they pull weeds. Our group's music minister, who got here six months before I did, calls them the Glory Hole, which explains why I like him and Mom doesn't. All of us are supported by contributions from churches back in the States, churches that like evidence of the good we're doing in the world. That's why I was home last week in Chicago, showing pictures of ninety-pound women lugging home gallon jugs of water from the well. I said, "We in America take so much for granted. Another well would revolutionize these people's lives."

Later a parishioner said to me, "They look so happy in their simplicity. I would hate to take that from them." Catching my look, she said, "I don't mean that we shouldn't help. I just worry about unintended consequences."

"Wise. But we need to think about the intended ones, too," I said. Next time I come I will bring a picture of Luz, my best friend in Bacoyan. Luz loves anything as long as it's electric. I managed to find her a Reddy Kilowatt T-shirt, and now it's her favorite garment. That would be a good picture to show people.

By the time the trip was done, I brought back pledges for $1,800, what Christian Outreach calls a good harvest. Also, I saw my old boyfriend. He grinned and asked if I had come back so I didn't have to eat goat every night. Mom always thought he was a jerk. I told him I was God's hands in the world, firm in my faith and gentle in my way. That got him to leave me alone, a story I would tell Mom if I hadn't already managed to pick a fight with her.

Goat, by the way, is good.

Coming halfway around the world hasn't changed me at all. Mom's industrial-strength faith was convinced that once I came to this village—barangay, to use the local word—I would finally see her God. I would see shining souls lined up and waiting for the hallelujah day. What I see are children with scabies that would clear up tomorrow if we could just get them clean, and young people frantic to get to Morlano, two islands away, where there is a jukebox and a fiesta every Saturday night.

"You're missing the point," Mom says crabbily. She doesn't need to tell me that she's regretting bringing me instead of my cousin Maria, a young woman already so devout that when two little hoodlums from her South Side neighborhood stole her cat, meaning to extract a ransom, she found them to say she forgave them.

"Don't you want your cat?" said one of the kids, outraged.

The road into Bacoyan is lined with palm trees that look like they're wearing skirts made of torn, tossed-out plastic bags, and goats shit everywhere, but it's eighty degrees here in the winter, the dizzying sampaguita blooms at night and floods the air with scent, and Luz bakes me pastries that crumble when I pick them up and taste like margarine and sugar and the rough local flour. I'm lucky beyond words. "Blessed," Mom would correct me. She's not wrong, but neither am I.

She's still sulking next to the well when I go back to find her. "Sorry."

"I'm going to have a bruise where you shoved me."

"Like I said."

"Do you think about the kind of example you're setting?"

This is low. I'm twenty-five, not eight. "I'm trying to keep their babies alive. That's a pretty good example."

She's staring out past me, at the path that leads to the church. Out of character. Usually she's all about eye contact, and plenty of moist hand touching, too. "I wish you . . . You're not . . . kind."

Why does this make me cry? It's hardly news. "I try."

"I know you do. That's why I wanted you to come here. I thought this would be the good soil that would allow you to flourish and set seed. But something in you refuses. Something there is hard, and will not be touched." She's never spoken like this to me before. Her eyes stuck to the horizon, she keeps talking, her voice oddly soft, as if we're having a conversation. Probably she's remembering the day Dad got killed, the event that drove her into Jesus's arms. I was fifteen when Mom went to the funeral home to see what was left of him after the boiler blew. She came home with clenched hands and new talk about divine messages. I swore I would be good to her, a vow I've broken every single day.

She says, "You won't allow yourself to be raised up. You're determined to look at the dirt, not the sky. Even here, in a place like paradise."

I lift my streaming eyes and see a smear of white shacks, a white dirt road, two nearby whitish goats. Above them the depthless blue sky, and behind them the placid, endless ocean. Of course it's beautiful. It will be beautiful until the end of the world, which Luz hopes to see from a well-lit balcony in Manila.

It's my turn to talk, but I don't have anything to say.

Because the horizon is too bright to keep looking at, I drop my eyes again, then laugh. Nestled at my feet as if I'd put it there is a dainty sampaguita, delicate as a snowflake, still open though normally the flowers close at sunrise. Nearby are a crumpled chocolate wrapper and a plastic straw. Now I'm really laughing. It's like Jesus's own irony. "Mom, look. Turn around."

She glances down and says, "Oh, for pity's sake." She sweeps up all of it, tucks the sampaguita behind my ear, and carries the trash away.

Haircut

Two days ago my daughter cut her hair off. She is four. She loosed a cowlick that now curls like plumage from the crown of her head, adorable. Everything the child touches turns to gold.

It seems impossible that she could be the sum of Larry and me. His crabs, my clap. His bad breath, my teeth. Our habit, which brought us together long enough to make Stella, and then wonderfully drove us apart. Stella doesn't know about him. Sometimes when Larry comes through town he and I see each other for old time's sake, when Stella is safe with my sister.

My girl is not like me. She reads already, and dances. I told Larry about Stella's pealing laughter when she, age one, encountered a soap bubble, and he said, "Cheap date." I haven't told him anything about her since.

He thinks I'm raising Stella wrong, and he isn't the only one. Janice, my friend at work, asked me just what I'm waiting for. "Kids her age go to preschool. They have playdates. You don't need to keep her in Fort Knox."

"I give her tests. She's scoring off the top of every one of them."

"What's going to happen when she starts school and finds out that she's not the center of the universe?"

I haven't told Janice yet about the homeschooling. I'll need to get my GED, which I started years ago and put aside when I didn't see the point. Now I hit the books after Stella goes to bed, pulling out sample tests on math and social studies that I hide in a high cabinet during the day. No point in raising questions if Larry comes over. But I've got to be nimble. Stella will catch up with me before I know it.

She stampedes into day care, racing to see her friends and kiss the stuffed moose that is her favorite. She was three when Laura who runs the place pulled me aside and said, "I think she's reading." Her long face looked worried, as if I was going to be mad that she let my brilliant little girl read when I wasn't looking. "I didn't teach her."

"I know," I assured her. Laura doesn't run the kind of day care where three-year-olds learn to read, but the kids are clean and she teaches them to share.

Stella can write her name and mine, and she draws the puppy she wants me to get for her. She resets the oven clock when we switch from daylight savings time, and she knows what daylight savings time is. She knows the names of our mailman and our neighbors, and though she doesn't run up to them—I'm careful about what I let her do—she waves and says hello. She charmed Adele Burgess one snowy day when Adele came stumping up the street behind her walker, scowling at the slushy pavement.

"The snowflakes are dancing!" Stella said, not her usual kind of talk. I thought maybe she was afraid of Adele, and so let herself sound babyish.

Adele was afflicted with everything—bad feet and swollen knees and skin that caught and tore like paper, and she met everyone she saw with a long list of joints that pained her, but this day she smiled at Stella. I didn't know the old bitch could. "You have quite an imagination!" Adele said.

After she was out of earshot, Stella leaned toward me. "The snowflakes are really just falling, but I thought she might like to hear about dancing."

GED sample question: *What is an opinion rather than a fact?*

"It's time for you to meet someone," Janice tells me.

"I've got a kid at home. Guys would rather start fresh."

"You have a pretty smile and long hair. Plenty of guys would give you a chance."

"Did I say I was interested?"

"That girl of yours is going to want a daddy. Or a brother or sister. Maybe you could get a car with air-conditioning out of the deal."

"Got my whole life worked out, don't you?" I smile, she smiles back. I have a better life than hers, so she's allowed to be bossy. It was Janice of all people who made me quit smoking before Stella was born. I've seen that woman go through three packs in a night, but she kept taking cigarettes out of my fingers when we were on breaks. "You don't want a dumb one," she said. Her kids are with their dad's mother.

Now she reaches out to touch my hair. "You can borrow my flat iron." For a treacherous second I remember how it used to be, with music and beer bottles and hot hands against my waist.

Stella is used to hearing about Janice the same way I'm used to hearing about Louis at her day care who won't drink chocolate milk unless graham crackers are crumbled into it. I don't expect her to think much when I tell her that Janice and I might go out some night, and Stella would be able to stay with her aunt and watch whatever TV my sister thinks is right for a girl aged four going on nineteen.

"Is it a date?" Stella asks.

"Silly. Janice is my friend. We don't go out on dates."

"But you might, if you meet someone." Her eyes are startlingly clear, the blue of swimming pools. "Louis's mom goes out every Friday. He gets to eat Pop-Tarts."

"If a date ever comes up, you can negotiate Pop-Tarts with Aunt Doreen."

Stella grins. She loves me to use big words with her, and I haven't stumped her yet, though as she twirls away chanting "neg*o*tiate," I feel as if I've swallowed a cannon-ball. I can already hear the scorn in Janice's voice when I explain there will be no night out.

GED sample question: *If a savings account pays 5% simple interest, how much interest in dollars will $4,000 earn in two years?* I have never seen $4,000 at one time in my life. I make up my own question. *If a pack of cigarettes costs $5.30, how much is each cigarette in a pack?*

Stella storms back into the room, her new cowlick bobbing on top of her head like a decoration. She's holding a book she brought home from day care, and her finger is stabbing at a word. "What is this?" she demands.

"Sound it out," I say automatically.

She can get as far as *b-a-l-l-*, but the rest stumps her, even though the drawing on the page is crowded with bal-loons and for God's sake, it isn't that hard. "Ballow," she keeps saying. Tears are coming to her eyes. She hates being wrong.

"Come on." I put her coat on, and we go outside, Stella not even asking where we were going. Janice is on shift, and she'll give us a balloon for nothing. Sure enough, her face breaks into a grin when she sees us.

"What happened to that kid's hair?"

"Ten minutes when Mom wasn't looking," I say.

"You want to get some scissors to even it out?"

"Nope," I say. "A balloon."

"Balloon!" Stella whoops, finally getting it.

Janice looks at her oddly, but inflates a green balloon

for her at the helium tank and ties it off with a long ribbon. She's ready to tie the end to Stella's cowlick, but I'm not having it. My girl and I walk home, her pretty face flooded with joy at the new word she owns, and all I can think of is pins, knives, scissors.

Rock and Roll

For the sixth time tonight, Jimmy yells "Rock and roll!" and jumps from the riser. He packs a good 240 now, and the stage throbs when he comes down. We're at a speedway outside of Versailles, Indiana, and I hold my breath, though maybe I should thank him. Dead because my idiot bandmate thinks he's Mick Jagger? Could be worse.

We crash to an ending and the crowd stops talking and balances their hot dogs and Cokes on their knees to applaud. Beyond the fifth row, people tilt their faces to watch us on the world's smallest Jumbotron. A Dinkytron. The seats are maybe half full, even though Run Dog Run opened for us, and they had a hit in the '80s. Maybe the Run Dog Run fans are saving their money for the next time the Stones come around. Maybe they can't make it from the parking lot on their walkers. Maybe, if I go out there to hang myself, they'll offer me a bite of hot dog first.

"Manny! Manneeeee!" Right in front of us, Row 4. Five of them. They've got glow sticks and a sign done in glitter that reads MEMPHIS MORNING, the lesser of our two hits. I stick a buzz roll in and they shriek like they're sixteen, which they haven't seen since Carter was president. "We're your groupies!" one of them said after the Dayton show. I gazed in despair at her double-knit pantsuit and white walking shoes, and she stuck out her tongue and grinned. They're loaded when they come to the shows, and they shout all our lyrics back at us. When Jimmy forgets words, he just turns the microphone to them.

Right now he's prancing across the front of the stage, pumping his fist and trying to get the rest of the audience to clap along while I hit the cowbell. He's giving it his all, and his hair streams behind him, gray, fuzzy, and two feet long. "Jimmy!" our groupies moan.

If one of us was stupid enough or drunk enough to even feel one of these women up, she'd probably hit him with her handbag. We are strictly the extras in the group fantasy these gals are having. When they drive home, they will scream with laughter, tease each other about which of us is hottest, and decide it's Jimmy. Then they'll pull up our next date on somebody's phone and figure out whose car they can take and what casserole to make ahead for their husbands and kids.

"Rock and roll!" The stage groans.

The band suffered its own group fantasy when we put together this reunion tour, teetering on two dimly successful songs from 1974, when I thought I had something to say, Jimmy had friends at WXRT, and girls actually did want to hang around and fuck us, for one night, if there wasn't a bigger star nearby. The whole thing worked when we could tag on to group concerts, and fans waiting for Aerosmith or Queen were willing to spend our set getting high. Both our hits were on *Phoenix in Flames*, the only record anyone remembers. The second album, *Dog Logic*, sold less, and the third didn't even get released. "Boys," said our manager, and shook his head. We were back on the sidewalk in ninety seconds, the shortest meeting on record.

The groupie with the curly blond hair is standing on her seat, waving the glow stick in an ecstatic arc over her head while Jimmy saws away on his solo. She's so drunk, it's amazing she can stand up. Jimmy—what the hell?—is at the edge of the stage, hauling her up. I glance at Rick, who is making are-you-out-of-your-mind eyes. Jimmy's got her up on stage now, and she's waving the glow stick in front of his eyes as if she can hypnotize him. I can tell from here that she'd blow 0.2 in a Breathalyzer. Jimmy pulls her in close to sing the last note with him, and she's within a couple of octaves. She glances around the stage, beaming as if she'd just won an award, and her co-groupies are scrubbing the air with their glow sticks. The ride home is going to be epic.

The groupie turns around and grins at me, running her tongue over her wrecked lipstick. Before I can respond, she's got her shirt off and is flashing her soft, collapsed boobs. The stage cam projects her boobs on the Dinky-tron, and for the first time tonight, the crowd roars. She shimmies, holding the boobs in her hands like twin Jell-O molds. Decent friends would be getting her covered. Her friends are whistling and pumping their fists.

This is all Jimmy's fault, but she's making straight for me, boobs wobbling in her hands. When she gets close, she twiddles her nipple, her eyes so glazed they look like melting ice.

The whole audience is on its feet, stomping and scream-ing, finally sounding like a rock-and-roll crowd. She's so close that my sweat splashes onto her floury skin. The first time I glance at her, she's grinning, but the second time, the grin is fading, and her boobs seem to be melting in her hands, and I won't be able to take it if she cries. I lean away from the drum set and do a bunch of nine-stroke rolls right on her boobs, keeping the strokes light so I won't hurt her. The song's over anyway; it's not like the band needs me. The crowd goes berserk, but what I watch is her face, waiting for the smile to come back.

It's like sunrise. Even her boobs seem to smile. She raises her arms and yells, "Rock and roll!" Nobody but me has noticed that this song is about heartbreak and the impossibility of starting over, "Memphis" a metaphor for what once was. I wrote the lyrics. Nobody remembers that, either.

She leans toward me with a foxy smile and gestures

for me to put my ear down to her mouth. "I'm going to be sick," she says, and then turns around and heaves like a pro. The Dinkytron catches every drop, and the cheers rock the rafters.

Rick has always said that no fans should be allowed backstage after the shows, but nobody before has ever wanted to come. We get the shirt back on the blonde, whose name is Nancy, and she stretches out on the cracked couch while her friends rotate around her. "How far do you have to drive back tonight?" Rick asks.

"Just to Indy. A little over an hour."

"More if we have to stop."

"There's that good all-night diner at State Road 38. It has clean bathrooms."

Nancy moans. Her face is white as a moon, but at least her friend dabbed the vomit off her mouth with a damp napkin. "She's going to need some water," Jimmy says.

"Bed," Nancy mutters. She looks like what she is now, every inch of sixty years old, with hips that hurt and a dye job that's giving out. When she first listened to us she had no idea how a life could dissolve, leaving you with nothing but your own sorry body. That's why she's here. I rest my hand on her shoulder and she manages a tiny smile.

"Don't go just yet," Rick says, clicking away on his phone. "I'm comping you all tickets for the Terre Haute show."

"I'm not sure—," one of the friends says.

From outside in the parking lot, fans are bellowing the

words to "Memphis Morning." They howl like wolves, and somebody yells, "Rock and roll!" His voice sounds torn, and it dissolves into a fit of coughing, but others—his friends—cheer him on.

"You did that," I say to our girls. "You're in the band."

L.A.

I was savagely cranky the morning I met my first single bride. My husband, Bill, had come home at 3 a.m. His job—he got *paid* for this—was to escort that day's new talent around West Hollywood and Silver Lake, making sure no paparazzo had the chance to snap her sitting alone or looking bored. Plastered, Bill had giggled when he tiptoed into the bedroom, knocking over the lamp and stepping on the cat's tail, and when I snapped at him he informed me that the new talent didn't whine. "I'll bet she doesn't," I said, and locked my mouth tight. While Bill snored all over the bed, I sat rigid in the living room and watched *CSI* until it was time to go to work.

Seeing the girl waiting for me at the shop's front door, I wasn't as kind as I might have been. She wasn't to blame for the broken lamp or the cat who was probably still under the bed, but when I said, "How can I help you?" I made the question sound like what I really meant: What the fuck do you want? She looked puffy and bruised, not the kind of rose that usually came into Monica's Bridal surrounded by a bouquet of cooing friends and cousins and mother, stepmother, grandmother, sister, neighbor, dog groomer, manicurist, and spray-tan applier. This was L.A., and people liked to pile onto each other's dreams.

"I want this." She held up her phone and showed me a disaster of a dress, layers of frosting-white ruffles into which a disdainful model had been inserted. If the soft, terrified girl in front of me tried to put on this dress, she would dissolve into hyperglycemia.

"That's special order. When is the wedding?"

"There isn't a date yet."

"How about a venue? This train is awfully formal."

She shook her head.

I tried for a joke: "You've got a groom, right?"

"He's coming. An astrologer told me to be ready."

For the second time in twelve hours, I closed my mouth before I could say anything more. The girl was trembling. We still hadn't stepped past the front door. She said, "I've looked at a lot of dresses online, and this is the one I want."

"It's important to see how a dress actually looks on you," I said, sinking gratefully into the honed-smooth speech. Bridal shops attract the floridly crazy, and at least once a month we got a girl planning her wedding to Prince

Harry, but this girl didn't have a fake British accent or a smile she flashed for invisible photographers. Nevertheless, she looked wounded, and I blazed with quick fury at the careless men I imagined who had created this shaking child. "Would you let me show you some different styles, just so you can see them on? We can take as long as you want. I want you to have the chance to be surprised. Just like your husband will."

"I already know what I want. But we can try on dresses if you don't have anything better to do with your time."

"We have all the time in the world," I said gently. I hadn't learned yet that the single brides don't need special handling. No matter how much they tremble, they are bulletproof.

I thought that girl was a one-off, bearing her sad, unique brand of delusion, until the next one came in a few months later, and three more since her, girls wearing engagement rings they've bought themselves and carrying fabric swatches and dye charts in their purses. Weddings take planning. Venues are sometimes booked two years ahead. No sane girl is going to leave the most important day of her life to chance.

"Where are you going to live, after the wedding?" I asked another girl.

The single bride shrugged. "We'll figure something out." She savored *we*, a pronoun she didn't yet have experience with.

Bill explains to me after every night he comes in late,

which is every night, how nothing happened between him and the new talent. It's his job to escort her and make sure her needs are tended to. It's his job to make her look happy in the brilliant Hollywood light. "You wanted to move to L.A.," he says. Sounding wounded is his long suit.

"That was my mistake. Now I want to move somewhere sane."

"What would I do there?"

Good question. L.A. fits him like an Italian suit. I'm the one with, he once told a laughing roomful, midwestern values. I grew up in Ohio, like him, and went to a university there, unlike him. We got married in front of a judge, which my mother said wasn't a wedding at all. I wanted to come to a city. Now Bill's the happy one.

"I don't want a June wedding," my latest single bride tells me. Her tattoos peek colorfully through the lace across her shoulders. "June brides are a cliché. I don't want to have to share my day."

This one's name is Isabel. Her cake will have musical notes made of lilac fondant. A backup singer, Isabel is looking for a groom who plays the drums, because drummers have great arms and are more trustworthy than guitarists.

"What will you do if you don't find one?" I say around the pins in my mouth.

"I guess I could go to Nashville, but we'd have to come back here for the wedding. I put a deposit on the reception hall."

"He might have his own ideas. There are reception halls in Nashville, too."

"This is my special day, not his."

For a moment, I think she's showing a flash of humor, but she is studying her reflection, her mouth firm. "I grew up in Omaha. I didn't come to L.A. to be like everybody else."

"You sound amazingly like my husband."

"Does he know any drummers? My psychic told me to ask everyone I meet."

"What else did your psychic tell you?"

"Ask for what you want. Otherwise you'll always be settling. There's no reason not to have everything you dream of." I'm kneeling at her feet, gazing up at her, my mouth full of pins. From this vantage she looks gigantic, a massive, frumpy goddess. "Can we let this out a little across the neck?" she says, and I nod and get to work.

That night Bill is actually home for dinner, a once-a-week event. When he comes in the door he looks tired, but in his pegged jeans and schoolboy blazer he also looks adorable, and about fourteen years old. I feel a hundred and eight. "We need to talk," he says.

"Do you know any drummers?"

"I'm not even going to ask."

"My client wants a drummer. She says she can have anything she wants if she asks for it."

"Ha. A million bucks," he says.

"Two million. And a Beemer."

"Quit thinking so small. A Bentley. And the house to go with it." He's finally stepped away from the door and poured himself onto the couch. It isn't the conversation he'd meant to have, but he's always taken opportunities that present themselves. It's why I asked him to marry me. I asked, and he did. "A plane," he says.

"Where would we go?" I know my mistake as soon as the words are out of my mouth.

"Who said anything about 'we'?" He smiles. The L.A. sunset floods the room in golden light.

Before

Like that, he was old. I didn't recognize him when he crossed the street toward me, my own father. He took one look at my face and put his hand, the scent and weight of a tobacco leaf, on my shoulder. "Oh, honey." That was before it got bad.

He used to run two companies, because one company was boring. He used to ski. He never once helped me with my homework, but he let me drive his Corvette from the time I was five. I steered; he worked the pedals. White, red interior, '61. "I never should have let it go," he says on the days he remembers it.

"It burned oil. You couldn't keep it out of the shop."

"Who cares? I had a Corvette. What do I have now?"

"A Corolla." Jesus, he should remember at least this one. He complains about it often enough.

His mind is like a canal lock, letting water rise, then letting it flow out again. Every once in a while a deep-hulled memory comes along, and I let myself be encouraged. He says, "The top of that Corvette must have weighed fifty pounds. By the time I wrestled it off, I'd have to take a shower. Your mother would glance at me and say, 'Taking the car out, dear?'"

"She loved it, too."

"She sure did. She'd wrap up her hair in a scarf, put on sunglasses, and sit in the passenger seat until I took her somewhere."

"Where did you take her?"

"There was a place that served Polynesian food. Does that still exist?"

I hurry upstairs and wrap my untidy hair in a gauze scarf, grab some cat-eye sunglasses and, in an inspired moment, Mom's old driving gloves. She said they made her feel like Grace Kelly. Maybe not the best way to remember her.

"Hot-cha! Where are you going?" Dad says.

"With you. We're going to test-drive a convertible."

"Oh, now." Suddenly he looks insecure, and my heart crumples. Not yet, not yet, not yet.

The BMW dealership is only a few miles away. I drive us there in the Corolla while Dad fumbles with his seat belt. Miraculously, he's able to connect the Z4 seat belt on his first try, and he grins at me rakishly. "Let's go, Pearl!" Who is Pearl? No telling.

The grin ebbs when I pull out of the parking lot, and

by the time we're in traffic, he's grabbing the dashboard and arm rest, his face white. I'm only going 30. I get back to the dealership as fast as I can at 30 mph, and he's sobbing with fright. The s.o.b. salesman who looks like he was up all night doing cocaine says, "A little more than the old man can take?"

"He used to be a test pilot," I snap, helping my sobbing father unfold himself from the passenger seat.

"Sure he did," the s.o.b. says.

Back in the Corolla, his tears finished, Dad looks out the safe window and says, "What state have you taken me to?"

"We're still in L.A. We never left."

"Don't lie to me. I'm not that old."

"There's the freeway."

"That's not a freeway. That's—When I was your age, I had girlfriends. You need to bring home your boyfriends. Every girl should bring home her boyfriends."

This is almost flattering. He hated my ex, recognizing before I did how brutally dull the man was. "Tell me about your girlfriends."

He shifts restlessly under the seat belt. The topic sentence is all he's got.

He breaks things—the electric toothbrush when it slips from his palsied hand, the blown-glass thimble that was the only pretty thing to come home from my honeymoon. In the light it looked like a green flame. "You shouldn't have left it on the shelf," he says when I come in.

"It's okay, Dad."

"Are you *crying*?"

I wasn't, yet, not really. The tears come a minute later when he looks at the floor and says, "Why is there glass?"

Every week I throw into the recycle bin pamphlets about health care, residential care, in-home care, outpatient care. My sister calls and says, "Decisions have to be made." Dad's old friend Lois calls when he's napping, and I tell her that he's fine, just fine.

The friend who actually visits is Jake, who Dad loves because Jake was a navy pilot and he now has a German shepherd. Jake and the dog hesitate at the front door, and I say, "Come in. *Please*."

At the sound of toenails scrabbling the floor, Dad's head jerks up. He rushes at the dog and I cry out, but before I can do anything, Dad and the immense dog are rolling on the floor, the dog's tail, the size of a baseball bat, pounding the floor, Dad's laughter round and huge.

Jake says, "I thought he might like this." His tears fall right onto his dark shirt.

For an hour after the dog leaves, my father is humming the Air Force Hymn, and then he turns on the news. It's a good day. "Where are my shoes?" he says as I'm setting the table for dinner.

"You've got them on, Dad. Planning on taking a walk?"

"Not these. My *shoes*."

They're his, all right. Ancient Adidas that threaten to

split any minute. "These are yours. Nobody else would have them."

"My shoes are brown."

"Those are your other shoes. These are your white shoes." I sound perky. I sound demented. I don't blame him for looking away.

He says, "Don't you—don't do this." In a split second, his face is tight, his eyes small and trapped. He had been so happy.

"Do you want to walk, Dad?" I say as gently as I can.

"Don't you. Don't *lie*."

I have to leave the room and splash cold water on my face. He used—never mind what he used to be. This is who he is. Will it be this bad for me? Of course it will.

From his room comes a roar, the sound of a very angry baby. I race to find him sitting on the bed, brown shoes on, untied. He looks up, his face wet and red. He says, "That place where you're taking me? I'm not going."

Spice

Out in the sun porch, every surface is draped and dripping pink: ribbons and wrapping paper and punch and cupcakes. A strawberry milkshake could have exploded in there and no one would have known the difference. The baby shower's been going on for two hours and we've all adjusted, but poor Rich, the father-to-be, stops in the doorway, pink-blind.

"Hi, honey!" his wife calls, waving so he can find her. "We're only halfway through the presents. Pull up a seat."

We're packed in, both moms and all four grandmas and Lindy's grad-school cohort and friends from high school and everybody she's ever worked with and me, the friend from college. She only wanted one shower, so we're here in force, including three cousins all well along themselves, displacing extra sofa space. I quit counting pink onesies at the ninth one, when the baby already had three pink teddy bears and a pink mobile to go above the crib. Like most of the women who aren't pregnant themselves, I'm nursing a strawberry daiquiri that's allowing the presents to pass in a nice pink blur.

"You're scaring me," Rich says. "If I stay in here, the baby won't ever have a brother."

"Then you have to stay!" yells Raynelle. She's the one giving the shower, and the only name I remember. "There are enough damn men in the world. Time for the women to run things. Down with the patriarchy!"

"We're cutting you off, Raynelle," I say, and the others smile at me, polite. The friend from college doesn't get to cut anybody off.

Rich shrugs and makes a place for himself on the floor between heaps of wrapping paper. "I've never been to one of these." He's wearing jeans and a dark T-shirt, and my eyes keep coming back to him just for relief.

Lindy's already ripping into the next present. The first few she opened delicately, but they took forever and her mother went to the kitchen and came back with a pair of scissors. About half an hour in, she gave up on the scissors, too, and just started ripping. Any minute she'll be using her teeth.

"Pepper and salt!" yells one of the cousins, responding to the shower game whose rules were explained earlier, when I wasn't listening. The loser has to sing a song. The current loser, one of the grad-school cohort, happily belts out "Let It Go," getting a lot of sing-along on the second chorus.

Lindy hasn't gotten to my present yet: a baby sling. I hope that the drinkers will be far enough in the bag not to notice that Lindy's college friend got her a hippie-dippie present, probably not safe to use. I remember, though Lindy may not, when we were nineteen and worked together at a food co-op, pouring fifty-pound bags of brown rice into open bins so the customers could help themselves. Once a man came in during our shift—not a member of the co-op, no one we recognized. "Guess you two are going to change the world, huh?"

"Guess we are," said Lindy.

"One brown rice cake at a time?"

"Think globally, act locally," she said.

"What if I don't want your changes?"

"Then you're in the wrong store," she said, and we were laughing so hard we barely noticed him leave, though our supervisor lectured us later. I bought the baby sling as a gesture to the girls we were then, and to changing the world, and to her new baby, but now she's an advisor to companies with third-world investments and I make hemp shirts and dresses, and could use another daiquiri.

"Look! Onesies!"

Lindy is not a glowy mom-to-be. Her lank hair drags across her forehead, and through the skirt of her jersey dress I can see the baby throwing punches. At this moment, Rich is a lot prettier than Lindy, nodding at the stack of pink receiving blankets and agreeing that these are going to be really useful. Rich and Lindy met after grad school, and during their first date Lindy put on Facebook that she had just met the man she was going to marry. I hoped she was being ironic.

"Oh, I *hoped* someone would get me this!" she says, holding up a baby-care set with a bulb syringe and snubby scissors.

"Nice," says Rich. Trying to be companionable, I reach for the present as if I had an opinion about scissors. He shrugs at me and smiles. I smile back. Nothing wrong with a smile.

"Pepper and salt!" scream the cousins, crammed on that couch like the see-no-evil monkeys. They're pointing at me and laughing.

"Wait. What? Why do I have to sing?"

"It's pepper! Gotta sing! Sing!" Even Rich, who can't know the rules any better than I do, is chanting along. Teasing, he bats my arm. Lindy has paused, the next present—mine—half unwrapped on her lap.

Her face is tired and hot, and I'll bet her feet want to explode out of their dainty shoes whose little straps are digging into her flesh. When we were nineteen, she wore Birkenstocks every day, and put her hair in braids. We signaled the end of our shift at the co-op by playing "Revolution" at top volume, so I launch in now.

Nobody sings with me. Most of the women look annoyed, and Rich smirks a little when I get to the part about everything being all right, which would make a decent lullaby. After two choruses, I can quit singing.

"There you go," Rich says.

"We're going to be here all afternoon," says one of the cousins.

"What is—oh!" Lindy says, holding up the sling, a little patch of unbleached muslin.

"Is that safe?" says one of the cousins.

"Mothers use them all over the world," I say. Every woman in the room is thinking that she lives in the United States so that she doesn't have to carry her baby in a cloth sling. I would understand that if I'd ever had a baby, had ever been pregnant, could comprehend the rules for a game at a baby shower where the father-to-be has become the honored guest. I glance at him, but he's staring at the sling as if I'd given his wife a dust rag.

"I didn't know people still made these," Lindy says, gently shaking it out.

"All over the world," I say.

"You're pepper," Rich says to her, and Lindy snaps, "No, I'm not. She's still pepper."

She's holding up the sling, surveying it. Rich's eyes slide over to mine and I smile at him again, but his eyes are assessing, trying, like me, to figure out why I'm here. It's our shared moment, and I try not to let my shame show on my face.

Lindy stands up, puts the sling on, and nestles a few onesies inside, along with a blanket that hangs halfway out, like a tongue. "It's not bad. It's actually comfortable." She smiles at me, then at the room. "We were friends," she says.

Learning

Our song just came on. Thinking of U.

This is not surprising, and neither is the picture of the flower. He thinks girls like flowers. "Our song" stings, but what did I expect?

That is the most lame-ass rose Ive ever seen. Ive gotta get a better class of boyfriend.

Ive been telling u.

When he texts me, he asks if we have beer. Usually he texts his girlfriends dick pics, but to this one he sends messages. *Its a great day. R u out?*

Hours pass before she texts back a video of an inquisitive chipmunk and a sprinkler.

Scott is so bad about his phone he might as well just hand it over to me. Love makes him careless, and he leaves the phone on the counter, on the coffee table, on the dresser. I can follow every twist in the plot. His girlfriend lives twelve miles away, and she doesn't close her bedroom blinds because she likes to see the stars. She likes sushi. *Bait*, Scott writes back. She's going to get bored with him.

Go out quick and look at the moonlight. The text came while he was showering, so I went to the window and saw velvet light coating every leaf. By the time Scott materialized, pink and damp, the light was fading, and by the time he wandered into the kitchen for another beer, it was gone. The next night he spent a half hour in the backyard, and when he came in, he had nothing to say.

She writes, *Did u see the frost this morning? Amazing.*

I feel like u r giving me tests I keep flunking.

Study harder.

He writes, *Do u love me?*

Don't think so.

Y not?

U keep flunking my tests.

Naturally I Google her and then can't think of anything except her videography business and her curly hair. I'll bet Scott wraps the coils around his fingers when they're pillow talking. They've been going strong for two months. Scott tends to fade at three, and I have the insane impulse to warn her. My other impulse is to put a bomb under her car.

She drinks martinis and wears tailored black pants that make the most of her ass. I don't know where to go to get pants like that. There's a silk blouse, too.

She writes *Change in plans. I've got to meet with my sound guy Friday.*

Lucky guy.

He's 6'2" and looks like Robert Redford.

☹

Use yr words.

There's an hour-long gap before he writes back *I dont like this.*

Two hours before she writes *Mama's gotta make rent, son.*

He sulks all night, drinking beer and grunting at the TV. I stand by the window and look at the cool light edging the honeysuckle that Scott was going to cut back two months ago. I give it six months before it swallows the house.

"It's pretty outside," I say. The gray light covers the lawn without illuminating it; this heatless light is full of possibility. "Come look."

"Why does everybody in the world want me to stand next to a damn window?"

"It's better than looking at the Raiders."

"Just please not now," he says. If I say anything else, he'll go to the bedroom and shut the door, so I wait a good five minutes before saying, "Look! A raccoon." He closes the bedroom door with a soft click. I made up the part about the raccoon.

The next morning, I tell him that I accidentally dropped his phone in the sink, another lie. I protect that phone like gold. He makes a show of turning it on to demonstrate that it still has a display, then disappears into the bathroom. He is reading the text that says her shoot went fine, and she doesn't like jealousy. It's their first fight.

He was jealous over me once—it's why he married me. He liked how I looked slinging beer in my Tailgater's uniform, and then married me so I wouldn't wear it anymore. After our reception he carried me over the threshold of his duplex, dropped me on the bed, and held me down by the shoulders. "If I ever catch you looking at another guy, I'll leave."

I think we got to our first anniversary before he started cheating, but I wasn't checking his phone yet.

The others have been just like me—regular girls, graduated high school, sometimes with a kid who becomes a good excuse when Scott's ready to move on. This one, though. I can't figure out where he met her. He codes merchandise at a loading dock, a job he calls "entry management." I've seen enough of her videos to know that if she was at the dock, she'd be shooting cranes and shipping containers, not Scott.

I buy steaks for dinner, and restock our beer. "Long day," he says, dodging around me. "Let me get a shower." His phone goes into the bathroom with him and stays in his pocket through dinner and after; when we go to bed, not touching, the phone isn't on the dresser or the bathroom counter.

The next day, when he escapes with the phone still hidden, I'm close to frantic. Frost furs the windows. She could be out with her sound guy again, or she could be doing setup for a new job she just got for the city. She could be with Scott, the least interesting possibility. I spend the day running errands, three of which allow me to drive past her studio. Bright, fat little beads of water dot the window where the frost has melted.

Scott is late coming home, and as soon as he sees me, his face crumples. "I——," he says, and that's as far as he can get before he's facedown on the couch, sobs clawing out of his throat.

After a while, I say, "Let me see."

An hour ago she wrote, *We're done.*

Not till I say so.

No response from her, of course. I am married to a moron. I write, *Sorry. Stupid.*

No shit.

Can we start again?

Y?

Im stupid, but I learn.

Ten minutes pass before *OK.* I toss the phone back at Scott. "That's how you do it."

He shakes his head. "I'll just fuck it up again."

I go over to the window and pull back the blind. There's no moon yet, but the weak, diffused light from the

neighbors' safety lights sparkles on the frost-tipped grass.
"Come over here and look at this."

Still crying, he buries his face in the sofa cushion.

"Come. Now."

This time he does.

Hope

I had never been on TV before, and didn't even pull a comb through my hair before I came out to face the cameras. As soon as the light came on I smiled, then begged the abductor—rapist, murderer—to turn himself in. My smile a gash across my face, I pleaded with anyone who might have seen my daughter, snatched from our broad-daylight front lawn, to call the police. "Please," I said, smiling. I was begging God just the way I'd been trained, full of confidence that he would answer my plea. The smile was proof of my hope. I was holding up my end of the bargain.

Jennifer had been twelve, Randy's and my only child. Investigators found the lawn edger she had been using tossed into the laurel. "The perp wanted to make sure she didn't have a weapon," one of the investigators theorized, excited to use his police word. Later we would find out about the maroon Honda CR-V with the plates that had been switched, and little girl five miles away who had been approached first, and who screamed like an air-raid siren until the CR-V roared away. Jennifer, a dreamy girl who liked gardens, must have fallen into his hands like a plum.

For weeks I kept the pleading up, praying without ceasing. I took my despair, which rooted early and which I refused to name, and twisted it into unrecognizable shapes. My smile distorting my face, I reminded God that he promised he would never abandon us.

Randy got quiet before I did. After dinner he sat on the couch and didn't even turn on the TV, his face slack as if he were made out of cotton wadding. Jennifer had chocolate-brown hair like his, and sometimes she joined him as he puttered in the garage. He would come back in the house and say wistfully, "She's growing up fast." He moved out after six months, though we are still married. The Lord once joined us, another one of his promises.

Even though we came in separate cars, we kept going to the same church, kept taking in faith's sturdy food. Pastor Michael, a good enough man who looked like he was drowning every time he glanced my way, urged me to lean not only on God's promises, but on my church family, my brothers and sisters ever quick to remind me that God has a plan and that everything happens for a reason.

They didn't need to remind me. The universe in all its glory quivers with reasons the Lord Almighty might allow a girl at the edge of womanhood to be abducted from her own front yard, where she was working for her Naturalist badge. Maybe God didn't like petunias. Maybe he was teaching me what happens to careless mothers. Maybe the sight of a twelve-year-old girl bending over to dig out a stubborn root was more than even God could resist.

"He wanted another star in heaven," said Theresa Mimford after we found out that Jennifer was dead. Theresa beamed as if she were offering comfort, and I felt my horrible smile stretch my face. So God can just reach down and take whatever he wants? How exactly does that make God different from Charles Louis Brown, parole violator with multiple priors, everything from DUI to armed robbery to, yes, of course, sexual assault? He looked at my girl, saw what he wanted, and took it. Maybe Charles Louis Brown, currently appealing his life sentence, was the hand of God reminding Randy and me just who Jennifer belonged to. Maybe I shouldn't see Jennifer's abduction as a tragedy, but as a demonstration of God's unfathomable love. Maybe I should be on my knees every day saying, "Please, sir, I'd like another." It isn't long before you start having thoughts like this.

We don't know where her body is. Charles Louis Brown, who of course insists he had nothing to do with Jennifer even though strands of her long hair were wound around the seat belt buckle, will not tell us where he put her. "She is with her Lord in Glory!" says Theresa. I hope so, I truly do. But if Theresa expects me to cheer up as I ponder Jennifer edging the celestial lawn, then she has a better expectation of my faith than I do. What I find myself hoping is that Theresa will lose something that she loves, so she can get a taste of God's heavenly food.

Wicked thoughts like these come wreathed in flame. The slyer ones are dull, voiced like logic. Mine isn't the only tragedy in the world. What about Lloyd Nathan, centered in the front pew every Sunday even after burying two wives and visiting his youngest boy every month in the state penitentiary for intent to distribute? He sings hymns week after week, full of pleasure in his Lord's crown. Or Tillie Forrington, her ALS far enough progressed now that she participates in the service only by jerking her head. I can see hope shining in her sunken brown eyes. Why aren't those eyes darting from side to side, looking for the cure that surely she's prayed for? Why does Lloyd talk about miracles when none ever came for him? We have been promised a banquet and served crumbs. Why does no one notice?

New words are boiling up in me, new ideas. I'm recognizing just what kind of God I've been worshiping all this time, and every day the impulse to share becomes a little stronger. Randy saw something in my expression the Sunday after Theresa got her breast cancer diagnosis; he grabbed me by the shoulders and steered me away from her. "Don't take her faith away. It's all she has."

"Then she doesn't have anything."

"It's not your job to tell her that."

Randy's voice was tired. His mouth drooped, his eyes

blinked too much; everything about him looked defeated, but here he was at church again, hoping in the Lord always. I said, "You knew, didn't you? Way deep inside, you knew there was never going to be a miracle."

"I don't know what you're talking about," he said, his eyes on his shoes.

Since he doesn't want to sit next to me, I sit alone for the service, studying Theresa, half shy when she lets Pastor Michael lay his healing hands on her. Her face is rapt.

I'm not a mean person. After service, I head for the parking lot. Theresa's the one who speeds up to catch me, grabbing me by the wrist. "I need you," she said. "Teach me. I don't know how to cope with stage IV cancer. How do I pray in the face of that? How do I hope?"

Her eyes, her whole face is shining. She looks like the glory of the Lord. I say, "Keep God in your every breath. Keep him before you."

"Will he save me?" she says.

"He will," I say, going under. "You can't imagine what he will do for you."

Breaking Glass

Not thinking, I mention the Year of Breaking Glass in front of Ben. His face tightens, but he doesn't pretend he doesn't know what I'm talking about, or doesn't hear the faint yearning in my voice.

The year was more like two years, on and off. Glass exploded and covered my couch or kitchen sink, and Ben's wife stood outside of my house with a shotgun. I lived outside city limits; we heard gunshots every day, but I'd never been shot at before. I'd hardly even been yelled at. I was aflame with guilt. It was thrilling, and so was the sex.

Shattered: two marriages, five childhoods, eleven windows, one car. Ben and I picked our way across rubble every day. Eventually we made a path, and the sex settled down. Since he came home to me every day, I wasn't thinking about him all the time. I was thinking about his wife.

After she cleaned out their savings accounts, she got a job at a Porsche dealership. Her father had been a touring-car racer, and had taught her some moves. Sometimes I sit in the dealership parking lot and watch her demonstrate torque vectoring on the closed track. The car makes a U-turn so tight it almost retraces its tracks, as sexy as a hand resting on the curve of a back.

Like every divorced woman, she dropped ten pounds and dyed her hair. If Ben met her for the first time tomorrow, he'd find out her favorite song and be sure to get her number. I know his moves. I also know how much he'd love a perfectly designed, perfectly functioning car. He likes perfection, as he used to tell me on milky afternoons on the floor of his classroom, the door locked after the kids left. When I finally go over to the dealership, I'm just saving him time.

"Unless you want to buy a car, I'm not interested in talking to you. And I know Ben can't afford this," she says.

"I make money, too," I say. Not much—I teach at the same school as Ben.

"The thing that puts Porsche ahead of its competitors is handling," she says. Her shoes easily cost $300. She doesn't bother trying to pronounce the heavy German word correctly. When she eases into the driver's seat to demonstrate the gearbox, her skirt rides up her thighs.

Ben comes home an hour after I do and pads around

the kitchen, mixing us drinks while I boil ravioli. He kisses me and I tell him to brush his teeth. "That bad?" he says.

"Could use a little freshening."

He pulls my head to his shoulder, using more force than he has to. "Love me?"

"Yup."

Zero to sixty in 4.3 seconds. I've been letting my hair go gray, and on the spot decide to start dyeing again. Ben comes back into the kitchen and breathes mint at me. I hold up sauce for him to taste, and he says, "Now it doesn't taste good." The gin does, though. It's been a long time since we had gin for dinner, and when the room spins we fall to the couch, not the bed.

"We're getting old," I say.

"That's been happening." I want to sleep on the couch, but he makes me come to bed with him.

When I return to the dealership, Ben's wife shows me the 911, so beautiful I can barely speak in its presence. "How do you plan to explain this to Ben?" she says.

The driver's seat is tilted back so that I feel cupped. It's enough to make me feel as if I've never been held before. "I have no idea."

"Well, that's your M.O." She must use something to keep her skin dewy. The blood of ex-husbands, Ben would say. I have an ex-husband, too, but he is not part of this story. The monthly payments on a 911, even with my income, would cripple us.

That night is Ben's night to cook, and he reheats the

untouched ravioli sauce. I sit at the counter, swirling my wine. "I have something to tell you."

"Don't."

"I want to buy you a car."

Relief arcs across his face. "What if I don't want a car?"

"You'll let me buy it as a favor to you."

"I'm constantly surprised at what I'll do," he says. He doesn't care for ravioli, and tomato sauce sometimes inflames his delicate stomach. We are near the end of the month, and he is concerned about deposits getting made. The alimony is a substantial percentage of his teacher's salary. He is convinced that his ex-wife is hiding income from the courts so that his payments remain high.

Through the bad time, through the broken glass, he told me that I showed him what forgiveness looked like. While I huddled alone, afraid to turn on the lights because they would show her where the windows were, I clutched the memory of those words. Now I sit up at night and watch TV in well-lit rooms.

The next time I go to the dealership I tell his ex-wife, "He and I drink too much."

"No surprise there."

"His blood pressure is high."

"Your problem, not mine."

"I dream of you waiting outside of our house."

"I've moved on."

"Those are happy dreams."

She revs the engine of today's car, the Boxster, and

says something I can't hear. When the engine settles down again, she says, "I shot out the windows of a cheater, but she was passionate. Don't just become a bitch."

"It worked for you."

She flashes some more thigh. "We have financing plans."

When I get home, I stand in the middle of the kitchen and drop a potted fern onto the tile floor. Dirt and clay shards and leaves fly. I'm dropping wineglasses by the time Ben comes up from his study. He grabs my hand, not gently.

"You're cleaning this up, not me," he says.

"What if I say no?"

He's thinking. My breath is ragged, my heart a frantic bird. "Christ," he whispers, and walks away. I haven't even told him about the car in the garage.

Sympathy

After the concert, we agreed that the kid, so skinny his T-shirt hung on him like a dress, yelled, "Jesus! It's called classic *rock*! Is that hard?" Half yelled. Strangling on its outrage, his voice twisted itself into a tight wire.

I said the T-shirt was Lou Reed, John said it was Led Zeppelin. He said the kid's hair was dark, but he shouldn't have contested me, because I notice things like this: it was almost white, an unhealthy, mushroomy color, like the kid lived in a closet. We were all in line for beer at a Stones concert, and the kid was at the brink of tears. The Coliseum speakers were crashing pre-concert "Honky Tonk Women" and the median age was sixty.

John's choice, not mine. When I got to pick, we went to clubs where you could hear ice cubes clink while the singer at the piano breathily crooned "Where or When." Median age, seventy. "They make us look young," I said.

"That is not a good thing," he said. "You used to listen to the Doors."

"I grew up."

"You're gonna regret that."

Did he think he could pass for twenty-five in that arena, wearing athletic shoes that gripped the metal risers and jeans that strained across his gut? The kid in the T-shirt spun out of line, gargling his anger, and rammed into John, knocking him back a step. The kid's eyes were all pupil, and tears washed down his face in a sheet. "What are you all *doing* here?" he said.

"Waiting for beer."

"No! What are you all doing *here?*" The kid had to scream to be heard over the P.A. music, but he was all about screaming.

"I love the Stones, man. Soundtrack of my youth."

The kid's mouth twisted. "They're not supposed to be a *soundtrack*. What's a soundtrack anyway, background music? That's a desecration."

John and I exchanged a look, surprised that the kid knew the word.

"It's music! It's the whole, hot—It isn't a goddamn *soundtrack*." He cocked his fist, but John caught the kid's skinny wrist and held it.

"Okay, son. Take it easy."

The kid actually started to dance in rage, trying to yank away from John and screeching, "*I. Am. Not. Your. Son.*" Just then the lights went down and John let go of the kid in order to reach for me, which is when the kid socked him in the jaw and raced away. By the time the lasers started and Keith Richards banged out the opening of "Jumpin' Jack Flash," the kid had vanished.

"Rock and roll," John said, rubbing his jaw.

It wasn't much of a hit, and we might have forgotten about the kid except that at the end of the show, during the din that you'd only know was "Satisfaction" if you listened to the crowd screaming the words, crowd surfing started up by the stage. The kid, maybe 120 pounds, was made to be tossed, and even from our seats up in row MM we could see his T-shirt flapping, and his sticklike arms beating against the air. "He's gonna get hurt," John said. "I won't cry."

The song shifted to "Sympathy for the Devil," and the crowd was roaring the chorus while Ronnie Wood shredded through a solo nobody could hear. The kid was getting flipped like a fish; a hundred camera flashes made him glitter. He raised his arms, and the hands underneath heaved him way up, flinging him into the dark auditorium air, where he disappeared.

A roar ripped across the crowd; even people who hadn't seen what happened were yelling. Mick stood at the front of the stage, his hand shading his eyes, rocking back and forth on his high heels. Then he shrugged and danced back upstage, and the roar from the audience got louder, and the kid was probably underneath fifty pairs of feet by now. Heat broke across me like a wave. "We just saw that kid get killed," I yelled to John.

"No, we didn't," he said.

"We—," I started, but he put his wet hand across my mouth. I could talk into his skin; nothing was going to change. I licked his salty palm. All of us were running with sweat.

"Listen." Keith and Ronnie were head-to-head, trading licks, pushing each other harder and harder and Charlie behind them driving like a train, the kind of jam you come to a concert to hear. Somewhere on the floor of the Coliseum, people were dancing on top of the kid.

After the last encore, John and I made our way out with the other ninety thousand people, our heads full of bees. When we got into the light, I could see the red mark the kid had left on his cheek. I wouldn't have noticed if I hadn't been looking.

We didn't talk going home. He was letting the music ebb out of him. When we were younger, we'd have sex before we left the parking lot, which was one thing music meant then.

When we got home I washed my face. He took the dog out. I stood at the window after he came back in, pointlessly looking for constellations. I have bad night vision, and can only see the North Star if somebody shows it to me.

"You coming to bed?"

"Yeah."

We had a good marriage. John knew I was also thinking of that skinny body, spitting with fury, sailing into the dark stadium air. I was the one who thought he came back down.

After John died, I kept the house. I don't go into the rooms that used to be his. In my office, I keep a small sound system, which is fine for me. I listen to Frank Sinatra and Tony Bennett. "Witchcraft." "That Old Black Magic." "Blame It on My Youth."

Ava Gardner Goes Home

1952

I used up all my capital for this: a visit to my sister's house at the junction of Nowhere and No Reason. Panic, which started ticking when I told Myra that Frank and I were coming, took over on the flight from Durham to Winston-Salem, and by the time we got to her house I was chewing gum and smoking at the same time, my foot rattling like a machine gun. Every building in town is a dull cube, the Hanes factory squatting in the shadow of the water tower. Frank never would have agreed to come if he'd had a recording session, a movie, a single foxhole he could hide in. But these days it's his wife who's paying the bills, and I get to insist on a trip that I myself have never made since I left

North Carolina with a bad suitcase and a drawl. I got rid of them both.

The whole town is in Myra's house. By herself, Myra cooked enough to feed the Tenth Battalion, and still everybody arrives with a covered dish. Four boxes are stacked next to the sink, each holding a red velvet cake. After the kitchen table was covered with dishes, my cousin balanced a plank on chairs so we wouldn't have to put food on the floor. Frank's eyes are darting around the room while he talks to my cousins, their friends, every salesman and gas-pump jockey in fifty miles. I need to get him a drink *now*. Me, too.

I say, "Betty Louise, just look at you! You could be a princess."

Betty Louise, who was my friend, opens her mouth and closes it again. She blushes and says, "Look who finally came home."

"I'm happy to be here."

"Bringing glamour to poor old Winston-Salem."

"It's good to be out of Hollywood."

"I can't think why."

"You're my people, Betty Louise." I try to hold her gaze, but she won't let me, fingering her flimsy skirt. If Edith Head had tried to dress me like my people from Grabtown, North Carolina, she wouldn't have come close to these rayon floral dresses in brown and green. Everyone is wearing their best. I think about the mink Frank got me and I want to vomit. "How's your mama, Betty Louise?"

"What's it like, in Hollywood? Are there"—her face goes so red it's almost purple—"*orgies?*"

"Not that I know about. Listen, Betty Louise—do you think there's any hooch around here?"

"Not that I know about."

Myra wriggles through the crowd to get to me, staring at my cigarette. "Ava, can't you get that husband of yours to eat?"

"Look at him. I lost that battle a long time ago." His face looks especially gaunt with everybody pressed up against him, the girls who want him to sing and the men talking about the war and then saying, "Oh, but you wouldn't know about that, would you?" He looks at me and I smile, meaning *thank you*, and he glares, meaning *you'll pay*. I glare back, meaning *you owe me more than this, you prick*, and Myra interrupts us, "Ava, look who's here to see you! You remember Dr. Milton!"

His perfectly round face glistens; sweat beads along the part in his greasy hair. Even though it's November, it must be ninety degrees in Myra's front room, and my tight dress lining sticks to my back and thighs. Frank's probably sweated right through his suit coat. Dr. Milton says, "Every time you have a new picture, I tell people that you sat in my chair."

That is clearly not all he tells people. His fat hands twitch toward me, and I flash my best smile across the room at my rigid, furious husband. "I tell the Hollywood dentists that it all started here," I say to Dr. Milton, then sight Myra's husband, Bronnie, on the other side of the cakes. Bronnie always knows where the bourbon is. "Please, eat, and help us with this food—I need to greet my sweet brother-in-law." Dr. Milton looks at his sleeve after I touch his arm, and nobody can blame me for wanting to wash my hand.

Bronnie used to throw mud at me. Now he can hardly speak. When I whisper to him about liquor, he swallows and nods. I glance at Frank, backed right up to the wood-paneled wall by men who are mostly, one way or another, my kin. He looks like he's drowning. I'm drowning, too, but I've gone to his damn mother's house often enough. Does he think I've forgotten the years he didn't get divorced, expecting me to sit and wait for him? And now we're married, and not even Hedda Hopper can count the times he's been unfaithful. She can count my times, and does.

Sweat is running in a steady line down my neck. There's no way to sneak outside without dragging the whole houseful with us, so I announce that city-boy Frank has never seen country stars, and we all troop out. It's cold enough in back to see our breath, and prickly sourwood leaves attach themselves to my stockings. In the dark I'm counting on Bronnie to get a flask to the men, which will work its way to Frank. "Get one for me, too," I told him. Myra doesn't need to know.

I keep greeting people, hugging the girls and smiling at the men, hearing the crowd around Frank getting louder.

He's acting, the Hollywood bumpkin come back to find what real America means. "Gee whiz," he says, and it's good that the darkness covers my face. And his. He's not a real actor; he's One-Take Charlie. He can drop into a character for a few minutes, but then it drains away and he's just Frank again, the washed-up crooner who still sneaks back to see long-suffering, sainted Nancy, the mother of his children.

Three nieces come toward me, giggling and shoving each other and pointing at my shoes. "Do you get to keep the clothes you wear in the pictures?"

"No, dolly. I have to go out and get my own clothes, just like you."

"Grandmama makes my clothes."

"Gee whiz," Frank says again.

Where the hell is Bronnie?

A hand rests on my elbow and I jerk away. Too late I see it's Myra, hurt moving across her gentle face. I press my cheek against hers, soft as powder. "Thank you for this."

"If Mama had lived—," she begins wistfully.

At that moment I have two wishes: to know the rest of her sentence, and to swallow a mouthful of bourbon. I can only have one wish, and Bronnie is edging around the crowd toward me.

"Sure," Frank says to someone, stepping forward and addressing the rake propped against the porch as if it were a microphone on stage at the Paramount. "Here's a little song people have been liking, ladies and gentlemen." Just like that, as if he'd planned it, he launches into "It's Only a Paper Moon," his voice so jaunty a person might miss the rage. Enough light comes from the kitchen window to see his gaze, on me at first. My nieces and cousins and aunts and friends scream and fall at his feet, like the last ten years haven't happened in Winston-Salem and Frank is still a star. His smile glints and he starts to sing to his audience, those stupid, shrieking girls. They are my people, and now they're his.

When Bronnie presses the flask into my hand, I kiss him, making sure Frank sees. That's what will start the fight.

Law and Order

Last week I went down to the precinct and asked about ride-alongs. The cop at the counter gave me the fish eye. "This isn't TV."

"I've got a son. He's fourteen. I can tell him what I learn." I dampened my lips. I don't have a son. "Sir."

"Any outstanding warrants?"

"No. I want to learn. I have respect for the law."

"Any of your relatives locked up?"

I made myself quit fingering the tie I was wearing to show respect. "No sir. Like I say, I want to learn."

Two nights later I'm buckled into the front seat, the AC set on high even though it's fifty degrees outside. "Vest is hot," says my host, Vance, who doesn't say another word to me for the first half hour. We crawl down some backstreets and he pulls over to talk to a surly young guy I would kick off of any crew I ran. You work construction, you get to know things about kids who won't meet your eyes. Vance rolls again, shooting the shit with other cops over the radio. We're coasting down an access road before he finally asks me what I hope to see that night. "There won't be no bloodshed if I can help it," he said.

"Good."

"You so bored that even driving a perimeter road counts as a big night out?"

"I've been thinking about bad choices and figured this was a decent way to see one."

"You telling me something I should know?"

"There's nothing to know. Believe me." My voice cracks, and after that the silence between us is a little softer. I'm not a criminal! And don't want to become one. "I don't have a son."

"I know. I ran a check."

"How come you let me come?"

"Most folks don't want it so bad. It's my act of Christian charity for the month." He doesn't look at me, I don't look at him. This is one of the things shame looks like.

He's right about the bloodshed, but around one thirty he breaks up a drug deal, some punk selling weed and pills he doesn't even know what are. The kid who slides into the back seat looks to be about twenty, blank and handsome and dumb as a post.

"You ever been arrested before?" I ask him.

Vance looks at me. "You a cop now?"

"Just trying to see what got him here."

There's a long, weighing moment, and then Vance says, "Answer the man."

"Nosir," says the kid.

"Did you know this might happen?"

"Yessir."

"But that didn't stop you, did it? Knowing what might happen isn't enough."

The kid raises his head then and locks his eyes on mine. "Nope. Your criminals, your bad element—they just don't think."

Vance whistles at the windshield, but I'm getting pissed. "You put the rest of your life on hold so you could get high for two hours?"

The kid smiles like a skull. "What's the rest of my life? A fuck-all job, kids to keep me locked in place? Sure wouldn't want to mess that up. Wouldn't want to trade it for something that might make me happy for a little while."

"Pull over," I say to Vance.

"What's your hurry? We're on our way back in."

"Just—please."

He makes a big show of driving as if the car is made of glass, but he eventually pulls up next to the curb. I get out of the car and try to open the back door. "Can you open this?"

"Fuck are you doing?" says Vance.

"Please. I won't make trouble." I can see Vance

reevaluating his Christian charity, so I let a little waver crack my voice when I say, "Please." Eventually he flips the switch and I climb in next to the kid, shutting the door behind me.

The kid slides as far away from me as he can get on the hard plastic seat. Doesn't matter to me—I know which of us belongs back there. Tomorrow I will go to work again, and the day after that. My manager, who shakes my hand like I have leprosy and who axed the only project I cared about, a halfway decent housing unit where a crack house and an extinct gas station currently stand, drives an Acura that I already keyed twice. It hasn't stopped me from daydreams involving car fires and kerosene. The psychologists say that if you've thought out a game plan for a crime, you'll commit the crime. Now I rear back and slam my forehead against the window. I do it again. I saw a guy do this on *COPS* once, but he was drunk.

"Grab him," says Vance to the kid next to me.

"Do it yourself, dude. He's not mine."

I'm dizzy, feeling great. The part of the window I've been hitting is getting warm, so I move to a cool spot.

"Christ, man, stop it. What are you doing?"

I glance around the seat in a small ecstasy of pain, looking for something sharp, but there isn't anything. I get in one more good hit before the kid grabs me.

"Shit. Stop it."

"I told you—no bloodshed," Vance says, driving fast now. "Don't fuck that up."

"No promises," I say, laughter bubbling up my throat.

"This here's a promise, all right. You hit that window one more time, you'll be looking at the inside of a cell, and I got no promises about when you'll be out."

My manager's mouth always hangs just a little ajar. In meetings I imagine sliding a knife in there.

Yanking away from the kid, I smack my head against the window again, closer to Vance so he'll remember me. Twice, to make sure.

Love

You were dancing at the tailgate party, and I heard people call you Lorraine. I was too shy to come up to you, but I have eyes. You look like another girl I used to know.

My brother-in-law has gotten sober, and it's like he's got religion. He always has the answer, no matter what he thinks my question is. The other day he said that once we turn thirty, our main task is making right everything we did wrong up till then. Sometimes when I think about things, the shame boils up my throat like vomit.

Lorraine, I'm sorry. It didn't come out the way I meant.

Love

I'm a grown man, remembering a girl he hasn't seen for ten years. Going over every memory, and then making himself stop, in case a memory can be worn out and then he wouldn't have the clamp at the heart. The worst thing I can imagine is not caring that once you turned your head when you heard my voice. Just that. You were happy to hear me, and turned toward the sound. This is pathetic. I know.

There is nothing wrong with a paying customer going to Greek Burger. There is nothing wrong with saying, "Hello, Lorraine." Don't make me feel worse than I already do.

When a person is lonely, everything he says comes out sounding like a threat. This is not a threat.

I stayed employed right through the recession. Sometimes I fed my sister and her husband. He told me that I should talk about the things I was proud of, so I told him I was proud to be bringing home a paycheck. I didn't mean it ugly. My sister said that not everybody had my advantages, and that made me laugh till I choked.

Driving home, I saw a girl who looked like you. I pulled up next to her and smiled when she glanced my way. She smiled back—a kind girl, like you. Then the light changed and she pulled away and I was left with my heart feeling like it had gone through the shredder.

No, Lorraine, you do not owe me a single thing other than correct change. I understand. But I didn't do anything wrong. I'm clumsy, I know. That isn't a sin.

She was right to leave. I was gentle around her, as if I was trying to coax a bird to come, but sometimes she'd glimpse a harder side, and I could see her step back. No one can be gentle all the time, and eventually I would have frightened her. If I could have had one more month with her, watching the light fade from her eyes, would I have taken it? This is how stories about domestic battery get started.

After enough time passes, memories aren't memories anymore, just habit. So when I think of you after I get up in the morning, it's not because I miss you—I'm just in the habit of thinking of you as my legs swing out of the bed where I sleep alone. My brother-in-law explained this to me. I picked up his Coke and poured it in his lap. In my truck, I turned the music up as high as I could stand it. That's my habit.

I don't go to Greek Burger anymore, because I thought you didn't want to see me again. If I'm wrong, I'd just as soon not know that.

For a while, I avoided your old place. I didn't even drive past it, so it took me half an hour to get home from work instead of fifteen minutes. I thought that I was being healthy. Maybe I got sick again. Or maybe I figured out that whether I drove past your place or not, you still weren't there. Now I drive past every day. When your sister sees me, she waves.

Mindy, the receptionist at the shop, tells me I'm a catch. "No kids, no record, decent hair. Just go to a bar. You'll be looking good." My sister says I'm attractive. My brother-in-law says I'm a tragic hero. I don't know who they all see when they look at me, which I wish they wouldn't. I look at myself and see a mug shot, even though I've never even had a traffic ticket. People can't be arrested for what they think, but maybe they should.

After you left here you lived for a while in Philadelphia, and then Connecticut, places so far away that I wonder if you're trying to get away from me, though I shouldn't think I'm so important. On search engines your name is still associated with your sister's, which makes sense. It's also associated with someone named Amelia. I don't think she's a girlfriend, but what do I know? It's easy to get a little bit of information. Every day I promise myself I will not look, and most days I don't.

It's not when I'm drunk that I look. When I'm drunk I whack off and go to sleep, which is why I like going to sleep drunk, no matter what my brother-in-law Jesus has to say. I look when I'm stone sober, moving from room to room and feeling the pressure of you like a tightening headache. I watched *The Avengers* over and over, and went to the condo gym eleven times in two weeks. But sometimes I look, just to ease the pressure. If I know where you are, I still feel a little bit close to you. I know something about you, even if it's only 1415 Stanley Lane.

Lorraine, I was not following you. It was coincidence. I live in this town, too.

Knowing one thing makes you want to know another. That's obvious, isn't it? Like Newtonian physics, which I spent half an hour reading about on Wikipedia. Energy cannot be destroyed or created, only changed.

After you've drunk all you can, and jogged through three pairs of shoes, after you've watched all the movies and talked to your family, after you've visited the animal shelter to feel miserable about dogs you're not home enough to take care of, after you've tried other women and shied away from the possibility of men, after you've eaten and gone without food and played *Minecraft* until your eyes dried out, after you've envied your brother his kids and your sister her asshole husband, after you've gone without sleep for a week and then fallen asleep in the Hardee's drive-thru, after you've rethought every thought you ever had and didn't need, after you've tried religion since you were on your knees anyway, her image might start to waver a little. There are things you don't remember. Maybe it doesn't matter that you can't recall her license plate. Your fingers, white from gripping, start to slip, and you see the hole your life holds, cut to her exact size. A thousand things could fill that hole—coaching basketball. Making beer. This isn't hard. You feel a light, cooling breeze brush the edge of your superheated heart.

Please respond.

Management

Teenagers twine around each other and complain to me about the lame music. Do they think I can do anything about it? "Manager" isn't the same thing as "Management" at Dogs 'N More. I'm the hinge on a greasy door that lets in frantic moms who can't control their kids, horny teenagers feeling each other up, sullen cashiers who figure they're too good for a hot dog shack. You come to Dogs 'N More, you get what's coming to you.

Which is what I say to myself every morning, every night. Me with my bachelor's in business. Me with the used BMW I'm still paying off even since it got sideswiped, because there's no way out of the contract I signed when I told myself a Beamer would look right in the corporate parking lot. I subscribed to *GQ* until seeing it in my mailbox made me mad.

My brother Randy was pissed when I let the subscription go. He had liked the articles about ties and protein diets, and he said I'd left him with nothing but daytime TV. This was not even close to true—for starters, he could try washing a dish once in a while. But he says that the sink is hard to reach from his wheelchair, and anyway, I'm the one who does most of the eating. True that.

I bought the wheelchair he liked, the one with a narrow wheelbase that he could maneuver. I found the one-floor condo with the accessible pool. We never talked about it. I was the one driving the night he went through the windshield and broke his neck. He was drunk, I was not. He had a nose full of coke, I did not. He grabbed the steering wheel, screaming with laughter, just when an SUV showed up in the opposite lane. It took all my strength to wrestle the wheel away from that SUV, and bury the nose of Randy's stupid Jeep in the post of a speed-limit sign. Randy was three feet deep inside a bush planted next to the highway. The city eventually billed me for that bush.

The bill sat with all the others on the kitchen counter. Hospital, convalescent hospital, doctors I'd never heard of. The ambulance alone was close to $1,700. "Who was operating the vehicle?" asked all of the insurance forms. In the end, I declared bankruptcy. When I was interviewed at Dogs 'N More, the supervisor told me I was lucky to get another shot. He could have been snotty about it, but he actually looked sorry. I appreciated that.

After work I stop by the grocery store and bring home dinner. I know what Randy likes—pork chops, fried potatoes, ice cream. Beer. I buy it, he drinks it, neither of us says anything.

On the weekends I've started doing a little construction work. I don't have skills, but I can carry buckets and mix cement, and we need the money. When the alarm goes off at five thirty on Saturday morning, sometimes I just stare at it. Randy's a light sleeper, and he hears the alarm from his room. He doesn't see why I need it to ring four times before I get up.

I'm bad at the work. Once I dropped a nail gun from a rafter, and no one has forgotten that. I'm soft on the shoulders and around the waist, and I get sunburned. At the end of one day when I had stepped in wet concrete, the guy working next to me asked what I was doing there, anyway. "My brother's a paraplegic," I said. It was the first time I used Randy as an excuse, and it seemed fair. He uses me often enough.

One morning I got to the site early. It was July, and the sun was already high, the sky blue and shiny as enamel. I stared at the clean lines of the rafters against that sky for fifteen minutes, until a crew member drove up and we started unloading the truck. "Nice morning," he said. "Sometimes it's not bad, getting out of the house."

"Sometimes it's the only part of the day that hasn't gone straight to shit."

He let that ride before he said, "I'm going to take a big guess that things aren't great for you at home."

"It's nonstop party."

"Things get better. Hang in there." Studying his clipboard with the day's schedule, he was imagining I had a wife at home, slamming around the kitchen, or maybe a kid who didn't want to read. He wasn't thinking about changing a twenty-six-year-old man's catheter.

It had been another nice day, pre-accident, summer tipping into fall, when Randy and I went to a party at a guy's house whose parents were gone. I was too old, already out of college, but they were Randy's friends and there was a girl I wanted to see. When she smiled her mouth quivered a little. She said no when I asked her to dance, but then she said, "Ask me again after the sun goes down." So I did.

"No," she said again, but she pulled me outside, where the sky after sunset looked almost green. The neighborhood was nice—every direction was swimming pools and lawns and clusters of flowers that looked like bouquets coming out of the ground. My heart was beating hard up high in my chest. Randy was somewhere inside, taking care of himself. When I kissed the girl, her mouth quivered under mine, and I kept kissing her.

Later, before the guys who lived there told me to take my brother home, she and I sat in lawn chairs, looking at the party going on inside. "It's like watching a TV show," she said. "They have no idea we're here."

"We could run away," I said.

"Maybe in a minute. Right now this is just right." Her fingertips grazed my wrist, a touch so light I could have been imagining it.

The air was sweet and warm, and I felt my pulse moving in me like a steady current. Lights were on everywhere—patio lights and pool lights and street lights, but all I was aware of was the girl and the dark, where I wanted us to go.

Snitch

I tell the newswoman the same thing I tell everybody: "I knew it was my father. I just knew."

"Were you frightened to go to the police, or was it a relief?" the newswoman asks. I wonder where she got the idea that those things are different.

When I was little, he took me to Disney and to the mall and to the beach. I would come home from school on Friday and he'd have the car already packed and running. He hadn't been home in months, and bills would be spilling off the table. "I hurried so I could see my girl." He had burned rubber across three states. Don't tell me I've never been loved.

•

These days I take Mom out to dinner when I can. We don't have a lot to say to each other. For a while right after the trial, we worked side by side, when she got me on in the Gardening department at Lowe's. That was nice in the spring when we got to use the sprayer on the long shelves of bedding plants, the bright buds like jewels. Then it turned summer and hot, and Mom—she was full-time—was moved to Paints. The plants went white and leggy, lost their blooms, then collapsed in their cracked plastic boxes.

"They would have kept blooming if you'd watered them better," Mom said.

"No one was buying anymore."

"You used to like flowers. I made you a garden when you were little. Your father rode his motorcycle right through it, then laughed and laughed."

"What did I do?"

"I didn't let you see till the next day, when I'd thrown out the torn-up flowers. He was gone by then. We tried to start again, but the flowers were never as nice."

It took me a while to find another job, but I made sure it was indoors and air-conditioned, and sometimes the manager lets me comp Mom's dinner. It's been six years. Time to move on.

"I have a daughter myself," the investigator said.

"Does she know what you do for a living?" I said.

"She's in second grade."
"She knows."

After the arrest, I stopped expecting to be invited to parties. Some boys, the grubby ones in thin pants, wanted to hang out, and after a while I said okay so I wouldn't be alone. One of them watched me brush my hair for ten minutes without saying a word. I said, "It's not going to be any more exciting than this."

He said, "I thought you'd be different."

Dad had a big nose and dark hair that hung straight in his eyes. He was fidgety, and I never saw his hands and wrists without crosshatch cuts, as if he scrambled through barbed wire every night. When I asked him why his hands were always cut up, he said, "Gotta feed my lion, baby girl."

Mom was bad before the trial. At off moments she'd pull me into a hard hug. She'd say, "Lisa," and then nothing else. I don't think she slept for four months. I slept all right.

Usually I didn't pay attention to stories about missing girls, but Dad liked rivers and he liked Sonics. The girl was found with river weeds tangled in her hair. The last thing she'd eaten was Pop Rocks. When Sonic Slushees with Pop Rocks first came out, I begged Dad to get me one. He made me eat the whole thing, and then I threw up half of it in the front seat. He would have told the girl that she didn't need to finish it. He learns fast.

"Your music is crap."

He grinned. When he was high, everything was a joke. "You wouldn't know good music if it bit you on the butt."

"You wouldn't know good music if it came sneaking in your bedroom window."

"Wait—you got any boys sneaking in your bedroom window?"

"Maybe."

"Tell them—Tell them you've got a dad."

"And that's supposed to scare them off?"

"It's supposed to make them careful. Then tell them your dad knows what good music is, and where to get it."

He didn't come to see me after he raped her. The state-appointed child psychologist said, "He wanted to protect you," like that was breaking news.

Police were all over this one from the start—first the missing girl, then the sketch. So many clues, I was ashamed of him. After a week, it was obvious that he wasn't coming home. He was with a girlfriend, earbuds blasting away. He was stretched out on her couch, soaking up her sun. Shaking, I went to the police station.

Mom won't say his name, or the raped girl's. She'll say, "Lisa—"

One of these days she'll figure out what to say next.

He taught me red-winged blackbirds. A man doesn't have to be a criminal one hundred percent of the time. He taught me times tables, too, smacking me when I started to twist and whine. "This is something you're going to need."

The only boy I liked at school was Alan Peery. When we were doing Personal Histories in health class he looked over at mine, and then on my birthday he put flowers on my desk. Five months later. He said, "I have a good memory."

I wanted to be with him, but he was just a nice person, not a player. I'd sit on his lap and he'd gently push me off, pat my hand. He wasn't gay, according to Hot Pants Heidi Connor, who would know. Alan was just careful. I knew better than to say a word about him to either Mom or Dad—Mom would be too hopeful, and Dad would hurt him.

I wanted the police to figure it out, but they kept going on TV to say, "No leads," and I drove my fingernails hard enough into my palms to draw blood. When I went to the police, my mouth felt like it was full of paste. The officer taking my statement had to keep getting me bottles of water, and I knew he thought I was high. It took forever to get the statement out. Then I left the station and looked both ways before I crossed the street. When I got to the car, I looked in the back seat, then underneath.

The detective wanted me to testify, but she couldn't force me. I was only fifteen. I told her what to look for, and when we were finished, she took my hands and thanked me. I never asked her to touch me.

I was surprised that Mom went to the trial. She came miserably home every day, dragging her shadow as if it were made of lead, and I wondered what man she thought she'd married.

"Do you want to hear?" she said. Some days I did, some I didn't. Her face got complicated when she told me that the girl was twelve, "younger than you." No kidding. That's why I went to the police.

•

Someday he'll get out. His sentence was fifteen years, and he's smart, he'll get out in eight, less. He'll come to see me.

"You still listening to that so-called music?"

"I've moved on."

"Not my little girl anymore?"

Smile. It's important not to lie.

"You've grown up, I can see that. You don't eat Pop Rocks anymore."

"I never should have eaten them in the first place."

"No," he'll agree, his hand light on my wrist. No need to think any further. Anybody knows what comes next.

Edits

No, I won't give your daughter an interview. No, I have no statement for your class. I don't actually care about activism and disability rights. I will not be your sponsor or your spokesperson. I will not sign your petition. Your enrichment is of much less importance to me than you think.

I had no say in my mother's books, and if I could have stopped them, I would have. The money from them supported my therapy, and many days I would have stopped it, too. My whole life I have been a role model. I would have rather been a fashion model, but crippled girls don't get that choice.

Reviewers loved to wax on about how witty Mom's writing was, and how vividly my personality shone on the page. Strangers would come to the house and wait for me to shine. When I was eight I said to one of them, "Is your hair supposed to stick up like that?" and everybody laughed. I saw Mom look at me and assess. Would it be funny on the page? Apparently not. It didn't go into the books.

I've changed my name, moved to Chicago, work as a data inputter for an insurance company. "You don't make it easy to find you!" sing my fans. No, I don't. That ought to tell them something.

"Things have changed so much," the fans sigh. "This country. When you were a girl, people knew how to do for family. They took care of their own."

"I like having an accessible toilet in my apartment," I say.

One woman blinked, then said, "I wish your mother was still alive."

"I know."

Mom is the one they really want to visit. On every page of her books, plucky Mom refuses to be downhearted when we face another hardship. She makes friends with politicians, she sets up clubs, she finds creative, crafty ways to make her own versions of expensive therapy equipment to teach me to tie a shoelace or hold a fat pencil. The Pinterest crowd would mob her now.

Five books! By a woman with a high school diploma and a stenography course. *The Wounded Lark, The Song of the Lark, Fledgling, The Lark Lives, The Lark and the Rainbow.* While she raised five other kids in the baby-besotted

'50s. She should have written one called *The Crowded Nest.* Her books never included the mornings I wet the bed waiting for my brothers and sisters to finish in the bathroom, where I needed half an hour to use the toilet.

When the first book bought us a new house, she moved her Underwood to the dining room table and kept clacking. Dad worked at the exchange downtown and probably got a lot of ribbing about his working wife, but her noisy hours at the typewriter got us train tickets to expensive doctors, and once they got us fifth-row tickets to *The King and I.*

I owe everything in my entire life to her and to her books, and that is why I have no interest in telling my inspiring story at your granddaughter's graduation. If she's so hot on inspiration, tell her to just read a chapter. All the good stuff is in there anyway.

I wonder what I would have been like without Mom to put me on the page. Would I have been so perky if she hadn't diligently typed out scene after scene starring funny, indomitable me? I might have been a little dullard. I might have been an ordinary child, who didn't think that she was somehow created for greatness because she had already overcome so much.

Often, in the long nights when it's hard to sleep, I imagine the shadow me, the one Mom wrote about. Her neighbors look in on her; she has a joke and a kind word for everybody. "I'd rather be a bright spot than a stain on your day. We have enough stains already."

For her neighbors' children, she has learned to make apple crumble and thumbprint cookies, sweets that look better when they're messy. Covered in flour and apple peels, that me hardly even remembers the St. James Theatre, where Gertrude Lawrence sang "Shall We Dance?" wearing a hoop skirt big enough to hide several Siamese children while galloping in Yul Brenner's arms around the stage. But the other me goes with her friends to see movies where people dance. She doesn't clutch the scrap of memory from one night's joy that happened sixty years ago.

Please don't start in on gratitude. Someone like me, who has to be helped out of bed and helped to the table and helped to get toothpaste on the brush doesn't have a moment in which I'm not grateful to somebody. Gratitude is an iron chain I pull from room to room, every link clanking. The sheer weight of my debt leaves me hunched over my rigid, spastic legs, a physical imbalance so debilitating it takes me to the floor.

The other me lurches debt-free around the kitchen and the bathroom, relying on crutches and grab bars. Plucky thing that she is, she hardly even thinks about her disability, except on the days when her hip seizes up and she makes the requisite joke about Arthur Itis. When her hands disobey her, she leans in harder to correct the crumble or wayward bit of handwriting. She's sixty-seven, not eighty. Plenty of good years left.

One woman who found me actually said, "I didn't

think you'd be so old. In the books . . ." In the books I'm
in pigtails, I know. In the books I'm adorable. Even I am
charmed by me. There was no telling what I might learn
to do. Every moment of the day was devoted to the life I
would have. Now, already, that life has happened, and my
mother isn't here to make it sparkle. Without her, I can
only see the long difficulty of every day. You, my friend,
would be bitter, too.

Right now the other me is walking—left foot, right
crutch, right foot, left crutch—into the kitchen where she
will drink another cup of coffee. It's only September, but
the first tendrils of cold are winding around the window
frames. She can feel it in her hands, sometimes too stiff
even to pick up her shoes. Her friends say that she should
go to Florida in the winters, but what would she do in
Florida? She likes the feeling of cold air on her face, and
has always welcomed a challenge.

Without warning, her hip pings and her legs give way
and she's on the floor. Now she's facedown on the linoleum, the breath banged right out of her. In a moment
she'll reach for a crutch and pull herself back up, but she
understands that her body has turned traitor. Will her legs
let her cross the street? Can she carry a plate? Prone on her
kitchen floor, she is filled with a trapped animal's rage,
something she's never felt before.

I replay the scene over and over, feeling a thrill every
time she hits the floor and feels the new wisdom fill her.

"You're not who I thought you'd be," my visitors say, and I shrug and smile. "This is who I am."

Now, in a moment of genius, I give the other me my mother's face and wait for whatever she's going to say, so I can change it.

Hello from an Old Friend

The impulse comes over me when I'm bored and out of sorts. Paul would say that it's Satan at work in me. Since I know what he would say, I don't tell him.

Looking up Marla from high school leads me to Jody, posing with two kids and a car. Her husband works for Union Carbide. Reading about her reminds me of Lisa, living in Mobile now. She has a picture of a magnolia on her website, and her husband works for the state.

Idaho is too far from Florida for me to go to reunions, but using the Internet is almost as good. In emails I don't have to explain that Paul surrendered to the call and is a preacher now. He'd been at Allied for five years. We lived in a two-story house with rosebushes when he came to me and said he wanted us to pray. We'd been trying for a baby. I thought, why not?

He said, "Lord, if you are calling me, I will come. Janine and I will serve you."

I dropped my hands and stared at him. We went to church twice a week and he taught Sunday school, but a lot of our friends did that. None of them were talking to God about service.

Outside, a jay squabbled at the top of its lungs. Paul took a few minutes to find the right words. "Sometimes at work I'll feel everything fall away. Or rather, I'm the one falling. I'm dropping and dropping, and there doesn't seem to be any bottom, and all that's around me is God. What is that, if not a call?"

His face was soft, and I could see the fear there, and who knows? He might have been right. The stupid jay made it hard to think. "I've never heard a call, but maybe that's one," I said. Nobody asked what I'd heard: a bird jabbering outside a window.

When I got pregnant a month after Paul quit his job to go to seminary, he told me this was God's reward to us. I still won't say he's wrong.

God proved to be a fruitful giver, providing us with six children as Paul's ability to feed and clothe them dwindled. "Couldn't you at least have been called to a nice, big TV church in Houston?" I asked when we moved from Eagle to Blackfoot. He looked hurt. His sense of humor had been the first casualty of the call, while mine sharpened right up.

The pictures of Suzanne and Colleen and Annie, who's now living in Connecticut where she says she can't get used to the winters, show women who have kept their figures and their faces. Their husbands have, too. Occasionally their posts or websites will thank God for some blessing, but mostly they're busy chronicling those blessings, which sometimes include skiing.

There is nothing wrong with going to the Internet and looking up the lives of my old friends. No sin there. But I'm left queasy with resentment. Sometimes I write to them, subject line "Hello from an old friend," and hear back "How wonderful it must be to live such a faith-based life. I envy you."

Try it. Paul has taken to saying, "What have you thanked God for today?" instead of hello. The kids make up answers when he's not around. "Thank you, God, for giving Dad bad hearing so he can't tell I'm watching rap videos." "Thank you, God, for making it rain so I didn't have to rake." I laugh. Be honest: I encourage them.

I had exhausted my list of girlfriends before it occurred to me to look up Richard. He existed in that zone that comes before dating, when boys and girls look at each other with terror. Our little Jonathan, age twelve, is there now. Maybe it was watching him that made me go to Google, chasing the other kids away from the family computer that the church is still unhappily paying off for us.

Most of my searches take a little while, especially when I have to hunt down married names. But Richard Volking came right up, over and over, with images. He is an architect. He is famous.

He has a house in Barcelona and an apartment in New York, and is married for the third time. In one picture his wife is kissing a cat, which makes me like her. One child from each marriage: three little saplings in a row.

I rewrote my message over and over. "What a pleasure to see your success! Our old days in Cool Springs must seem far away from you now. I just wanted to reach out and say hello, and send blessings." The last two words are Paul's usual sign-off.

There was so much to do. Mary's homework, Esther's soccer practice, visits to Mrs. Berry and Mrs. Polkman. Cookies for the soccer team, the children's choir, Jonathan's homeroom. In a typical week I make eight batches of cookies, and Paul and I are soft as bread dough.

By the time I got back to the computer I was almost not thinking about Richard.

"You're right—those days do feel very far away, and so I'm especially glad that you reached out. I haven't been back to Cool Springs since Mother died, but I remember it clearly. The long willow branches hung like a girl's hair. No willows in Barcelona."

I skimmed the rest. Esther asked if she could have a cookie, and I said roughly, "Take them all."

Paul was late home from church, and when he finally got in, his mouth was full of words. His blessing before dinner clocked ten solid minutes. He wouldn't feel the need to voice so many thanks if he had prepared the food congealing in front of him. "For the blessings of Esther's soccer team's win. For Jonathan's homeroom teacher, Lord, we thank you. Our hands are your hands in the world, Lord, our faces your face. Bless our hands and faces."

He lifted his eyes and smiled. Wordless, I smiled back. The lasagna was a mouthful of rubber.

Now that Paul has gone to bed, I stay up and look at the computer's screen saver for a long time: a picture of a seagull and "Enter his gates with thanksgiving and his courts with praise." Josh set it up to please his father; I'm pretty sure there was another one he shared with his siblings that had a different quote. When the computer came into the house Paul blessed it, asking that it be used to serve and praise God. I am willing to think that looking up cookie recipes or helping Mary with a history paper are both service and praise.

"Dear Richard, I pray that God will continue to send blessings upon you, your work, your children and your wives." That ought to do it.

In the kitchen, I splash ice water on my face, which is God's face, over and over. It's supposed to keep us from crying. It's done it before.

Cat

My mother's thick hair tumbles over her shoulders, and her body is as taut as a heron's. She is making her way across hot Piazza San Marco with quick, annoyed steps, sliding past pods of noisy tourists and vendors. If someone asks her a question, she will answer in Italian, which I do not understand.

It's rare to be able to watch her, and I'm staring from my spot across the plaza. The sizzling wind molds her skirt to her long legs, her blouse to her shoulders. Her face is flawlessly impatient. She could be on her way to an assignation. She could be preparing to buy oranges. Before she is halfway across the dazzling square, a man steps in her way. She listens to him for a moment, then continues walking. He puts his hand on her arm, and she shakes him off as if she were shaking off rain. He is still talking.

People watching laugh. He catches up with her and grabs her silky skirt at the waist, leaving a mark. I stand up to go to her, my chair's aluminum legs stuttering on the flagstones.

Before I can get close, a second man arrives—tall, like her, holding a necklace that catches the light. She dismisses him, too, with a hissing sentence. Her calf muscle flexes as she drums her high heel—Milanese shoes, invoking raw silk blouses and high-strung sports cars. Though I'm close now, she doesn't glance at me. Only when a third man arrives tethered to an animal on a leash does my mother stop looking angry. The animal is a cougar, maybe, or an ocelot. Its muscular tail is almost as thick as my wrist, and swings as if scanning for prey. The cat shows no interest in the people around it, even the sticky-handed child following too close behind. This cat could take off one of those hands with an indifferent swipe of a heavy, soft paw.

My mother nods at the cat. She looks barely tamed herself, her body an undulant muscle in the brilliant sun. It isn't right for me to look at her like this, but for years I've wanted to see her palm back her rich hair.

Her hair was thin. She spent a lifetime struggling with it.

The man with the necklace is talking again in an urgent voice. Maybe his family is about to be displaced or his son let out of prison. My mother is more interested in the cat, and does not change her expression when the animal leaps up and knocks the necklace from the man's hands, a careless claw raking the inside of his wrist. An instant holds before his arm jets blood, spraying his face and linen shirt. The cat tastes the necklace, then drops it to the flagstones. The man wails, and two horrified women rush toward him. My mother turns to the man holding the cat's leash. "*Prosimmo?*" she says, as if a conversation has been interrupted. "*Di che cosa hai bisogno?*" I am furious not to know what she is saying.

The blood of the collapsed man froths over his arm, but all I care about is the cat batting the glittering necklace over the hot gray flagstones. I have to force myself not to reach out as if to a tabby. My mother says something sharp and the animal rumbles deep in its throat; I don't know whether it is pleased or the opposite, but my mother speaks again, heedless.

She was famous for her softness—her body, her voice. The men who liked her liked whipped cream desserts and approved of a woman who would order the first dish on the menu. "Anything is fine, really. There's nothing I especially want." By the time I was five years old I'd learned that wanting nothing was the same as wanting everything. "Either the veal or the chicken. I don't want anything special," she'd say, and I felt her want something much more than veal or chicken. I brought her bouquets when I was a little girl, and then, as the years passed, books, pictures, food, clothes, a car. "How nice," she said every time. I should have brought her a cat.

In Venice, my mother says something curt and takes

the leash. The cat is carrying the necklace in its mouth, the jeweled end hanging out like a mouse tail. The first man, who left the mark on her skirt, starts talking again. I don't need to speak Italian to know he is repeating himself, dejected. Whatever he wants, it will not be coming.

My mother turns for the first time toward me. "And you?"

"That." I nod at the cat. My mother shrugs, but she can't be surprised. "I have always loved animals," I tell her, and for the first moment she looks indecisive. I say, "Do you know who I am?" She smiles, snaps her fingers, and the cat looks at me, growling and tensing before it jumps at my face.

She is dead, and I can imagine her any way I want.

Nobody Happy

When I was a teenager, I heard a woman propose to a man in the parking lot of Ralphs grocery store. It was spring and they were sitting in a convertible. Next to the cart corral, I stood rooted, my hand clamped around the plastic bar on the cart. "I love you," she said, her voice stringy with fear. "I want to wake up every morning and see you."

Asphalt burning through my flip-flops, I held my breath. I didn't know whether I was pulling for him or her, but I wanted somebody to be happy. He didn't say anything for a long time, and when he finally did, it was, "Let's go home." Nobody happy.

Nobody Happy. That would make a good song title for a good songwriter.

I'm a bad songwriter, so I sing. That's the way it goes with music. Cole Porter could put a lifetime's worth of agony into one line that somebody else would deliver, and it would be a funny line. "Cole Porter was a fruit," Frank Sinatra said, and he then he sang "So in Love" with tears in his eyes.

I don't cry, but I know how to do tempos and phrasing, how to sound confident when my voice surrounds a note. Give me somebody else's words and you'll swear you can hear my heart breaking. Give me a piece of paper, a pencil, and all afternoon, and you'll get some cartoon cats, a list of words that rhyme with *moon*, and a hole on the page where I kept erasing the stupid lines, the ones I'm good at. I'll keep trying until I write one good one. That's all. One song to make the world remember me. I can't decide whether that's asking for a lot or not nearly enough.

Then it's time to put on my tux and do my show. Sometimes I go onstage with a highball glass of apple juice, pretending it's whiskey, like Dean Martin. Everything I do is fake—the orchestra arrangements that steal from Nelson Riddle, the soft approach on a note like Mel Tormé, the goddamn lapels on my tux that I tell the tailor to keep slim.

"What do you want to look like, it's 1956?"

"Bingo."

The part in my hair is sharp as a razor and my shave is paper clean. I sing at nightclubs that have 1956 wallpaper and 1956 coat-check girls. At every set there's at least one guy who's splashed out big money to take his wife—face-lift, heavy diamonds—to hear music the way it's supposed to be. When I experiment with a tempo, I get summoned by the guy and his wife. "That is not how Tony Bennett sang it. You're a kid. Don't try to improve."

I spent the better part of a month on a song that rhymed *improve* with *disapprove*, before I realized that the whole song stank.

I've forced myself to finish a few songs that seemed good while I was writing them. The next day I'd see the obvious lines, the predictable progressions. Nobody should write a song unless he has something to say, and what I have to say is that I wish I could write a decent song.

Once, after a girlfriend left, I gave up sleep and wrote one bad song after another about empty beds and lonely breakfasts. I thought that if I just kept writing, something good would break through, like a superhero crashing through the flimsy wall of a movie set. Whatever talent I've got isn't a superhero. My talent is a kid with his nose flattened against the toy-store window, wanting what he can't have.

Lorenz Hart said that he could have been a genius. You get to say that when you're a genius. Billy Strayhorn was black, gay, and anguished, and wrote songs so sophisticated we're still scrambling to catch up. In photographs he looks happy enough, like me. Why isn't my anguish good enough?

After a show, there's always somebody to meet—somebody my manager wants to remember me, one of Johnny Hartman's arrangers' grandkids, a hipster boy spinning vinyl who wants to talk about outtakes. "That's for the scholars," I say. I'm not much of a drinker, but these people turn me into one.

This time it's a woman, red hair a waterfall down her back. She tells me she's a cabaret singer and I start looking for the exit. "I do just enough Great American Songbook to keep the doors open," she says while we're still shaking hands. "After that, I'm looking for new material."

"Tough sell." I start a countdown to see if I can get from ten to one before she admits that she has written some songs herself.

"Audiences come in thinking they want to hear 'Stella by Starlight.' They just need to be exposed to more." Seven. Six. She smiles. "I hear you've got some songs."

"Where did you hear that?"

"Okay, I didn't hear. But doesn't everybody?"

She coaxes me over to the piano where I play her the chorus of the song that sent my girlfriend out the door, the one about sunset. It's so bad, I can't even make myself play into the verse.

"That's beautiful."

"Glad you like it."

Three. Two. "I write songs, too."

At that point there's no choice but to stand up and offer her the piano bench. Her song starts with a line about how blue can be the sky, but also the ocean. Girl, there's a reason audiences want to hear Duke Ellington. She stops at the bridge and says, "It's not as good as yours."

"Sure it is."

"I know it's not a song for the ages, but there's room for the little ones, you know? The small moments need songs, too." She plinks around while she talks, replaying what she just played. Her song is about walking on the beach.

She's waiting for me to say something, and the longer the moment extends, the more unhappiness creeps into her eyes. It spreads toward me like a stain, and just to stop it I say, "You really know how to put a song across."

There's the smile. "Let me play you one more. It's the one audiences love, about how people who belong together find each other." It starts with exactly that line and plods on from there, one blocky, over-earnest line following the next just like in any song of mine.

As soon as she finishes, she turns to me, her eyes round and moist. I lean over the piano bench and kiss her, running my hands down her back until I feel her relax and know she won't ask me how I like her song.

When she straightens up and pushes back her hair, she half smiles and half coughs and says, "Well. That was not a small moment." How many times has she said this before? It takes practice to make a delivery sound effortless.

She gets a spark in her eye, and I'm thinking, *Don't, don't, don't.* "We can make beautiful music together," she says.

I can't stop the wince, and to her credit, she winces, too. "I know. Cheesy. But still—you want to get a drink?"

I'm already straightening my coat, moving toward the door, so sorry, already, plans. She's got her own lines braiding around mine, too bad, next time, so great. Everybody knows this duet. But where is the song about the missed disaster, the shipwreck that didn't happen?

Shipwreck. Flyspeck. Breakneck.

Disaster. Plaster. Faster.

Soup (1)

Michael

Sunny arrived the day before my wife, Laurie, started chemo. She'd already had surgery that took away her ovaries and her uterus; the chemo was, her oncologist said, "to clean house." Laurie posted a Facebook update, and inside two hours Sunny was at the house with a basket of gifts—special lip balm because chemo does such a job on moist tissue; vitamin E lotion for her arms after all the needle sticks; hot pink socks that didn't look like sickroom clothes. I don't know how she knew what Laurie would need. Sunny was as new to this as we were.

From work, I called home throughout the day to make dumb jokes or ask what Laurie wanted for dinner, though I already knew she didn't want anything. Sometimes

Laurie would say, "Sunny's here," and I'd hold off telling her I loved her, suddenly shy over the telephone. One day Sunny answered the phone and ice ran through me, but she only said that she happened to be close to the phone, and then she handed it over to Laurie. Sunny answered all the time after that.

Laurie and I never asked Sunny to come; she just came. She spent her nights at home researching side effects of Taxol versus Taxotere, and came with us to oncology appointments armed with questions. "Are you a family member?" the doctor asked.

"Almost," Laurie said.

"Just a friend," Sunny said, smiling down at her folded hands.

"Quite a friend," the doctor said, his voice scrubbed of emotion or judgment, so I heard emotion and judgment. What did he care if we came in with a clown car full of people? I wished he would stick to the subject.

The subject, when the subject is cancer, takes over the room. Protocols, test studies, carboplatin, neuropathy, IP, IV. Sores, rashes, nausea. Percentages. After the initial consult we didn't once mention our plan to raise chickens in the backyard for the children we now were not having. At a working lunch somebody ordered chicken salad, and I had to go outside and spend five minutes getting a grip on myself.

"You didn't see it coming?" people ask, as if they themselves would have hidden in a safe interior room

with plenty of batteries and bottled water. Laurie and I
played tennis the day before the diagnosis and she beat
me, straight sets. She had gone for her annual physical and
something funny showed up in the blood work. That was
all. No tiredness, no distension of the belly, no weight loss.
Laurie would have been overjoyed with some weight loss,
at first. The joke everybody makes.

Even the oncologist sat there looking at Laurie's chart
and shaking his head. "Sometimes it happens like this,
like lightning out of a blue sky. I'm so sorry."

Then home, then tears, then phone calls and emails
and people I'd barely heard of, friends of Laurie's from
work or tennis club. Then Sunny. She had been at Laurie's
company, and they still got together a few times a year for
lunch or a movie. She was just a name my wife mentioned
from time to time.

The first time Sunny called me at the office and asked
me to bring home dinner, I was happy to help. I couldn't
expect her to make dinner for us every night. The second
time, she told me which Thai takeout place to go to for
hot and sour soup. When I got home she had washed and
folded all the sheets, which surely was worth some tom
yum goong. "You didn't ask for fish sauce?" Sunny said,
rummaging through the bag.

She was my wife's best friend now.

Laurie's descent wasn't even. She would level out for
weeks at a time, when we would tell each other that she had
hit bottom, and this round of sores and invisible, agonizing

pain was the worst, and suddenly she would be much worse, as if she had been clinging to the side of a well and was losing purchase. She slept so lightly that I was afraid to fall asleep myself; some errant twitch or snore could wake her from her wan rest. Sunny said it would make sense for me to sleep in the guest room, and she was right, but I wasn't about to sleep in the room for strangers, where Sunny often left her bag of knitting. Instead I got a cot and pushed it next to Laurie's bed. At night I rolled as close as she could bear and breathed her smell, now a sour mix of chemicals and the nausea that was at best partially controlled.

I couldn't begin to feel what she was going through. Sunny told me this before launching into a list of Laurie's symptoms and complaints, the intimate details Laurie herself didn't tell me. Sometimes bowel discharge came through her vagina. Sunny had to change the sheets several times a day. Laurie had bought those sheets, and even though they cost the earth, she assured me she had gotten a deal. She taught me that sheets could be special.

Sunny's coffee drinks in the refrigerator. The TV tuned to Sunny's channel. She liked to watch talent shows and set the kitchen radio to a classical station that I changed every morning so I could hear the news.

Today I come home with the Italian wedding soup Sunny stipulated and hear Laurie's laughter pealing from the bedroom. It's been months. I hurry in to find Sunny sitting on the bed, the two of them looking at our wedding album.

Soup (1)

"Memory Lane!" Laurie says. Her face is shining, and if Sunny hadn't been there, I would have kissed my wife.

"That was some haircut," Sunny says to me.

"It wasn't that bad," I protest.

"Honey, it was awful, but I married you anyway."

"What prompted this?"

"I wanted one moment in this house that wasn't about being sick."

My smile falls off my face, but Laurie is back to looking at my haircut and doesn't notice.

Since they look comfy on the bed, I go to the kitchen and put together a tray with soup and grapefruit juice—Laurie likes it now—and a rose from outside in a bud vase. Sometimes a rose makes her smile. From the bedroom comes another whoop of laughter, and for a piercing moment, I wish I could bring Laurie a glass of wine.

"What is it this time?" I say at the doorway, after pausing to get my voice right.

"Look at your *face*! Talk about a thousand-yard stare. You look like you just got a death sentence." She holds up a picture of us at the altar, and she's right—my eyes seem focused on something far away and frightening. I tighten my grip on the tray and set it gently over my wasted wife, willing her to look up and meet my eyes. Which she does, briefly.

Soup (2)

Sunny

Both of us jerk a little when we hear his car in the driveway. I've seen Laurie do it in her sleep—the slight tightening, the unconscious smoothing of the mouth—and I know she's dreaming of him. It's not something to discuss.

I'm getting as sensitive as Laurie, and when he comes in I can smell his lunch burrito and the Sharpie ink that has bled onto his fingers. Next to the bed he stands awkwardly, still holding his briefcase. Since the time she winced when he picked up her hand, he doesn't touch her, but he asks her how today was. "A little better," she says when it wasn't too bad; "a little worse" when it was a lot worse. I'm not saying that she's a hero. She's just sick of questions.

He has nothing but questions, and she understands

that. How is he supposed to know, if he doesn't ask? She does the same thing. "How was the phone conference? How did the meeting with Mitch go?" She closes her eyes while he answers, and then he tiptoes out of the room. In grief, his face is like a joint wrenched out of its socket. I ask if he remembered to bring home soup. There's nothing wrong with that. We need soup.

We need more soft bedding; everything now is hopelessly stained. We need better antiemetics. We need blackout shades in the bedroom. We need a decent place for me to sleep. We need a miracle, and somebody to say so. It's not going to be him.

"He wishes you weren't here," Laurie said once, after he left for work.

"I know."

"So do I," she said. That shocked me, and I started to protest, but she grinned at me and winked. "He wouldn't let me say that. He thinks it's rude. He loses track of what's important."

"No shit," I said.

Was that before or after I started going with them to appointments? I should keep a journal that I'll be able to refer to one day while I write about these muffled, beautiful days. *Muted Light: A Friend's Journey with Cancer.*

You say "friend" and "caretaking" and people assume a relationship that stretches back to kindergarten, memories of camp and proms and first cigarettes. I don't know why a friendship that started at the office basement vending machine is less legitimate. The first month Laurie and I knew each other, all we talked about was Cheetos. Before she got sick, I didn't know her husband's name. I heard cancer and I came.

Laurie caught me by the hand once. Even that small exertion just about undid her. "In case he doesn't say it, thank you."

"Of course he says it."

She gave me a look that bundled up *Oh, come on* with *Don't make me say it.* She's perfected communication with a twist of the mouth and a tilt of the head; sometimes we go through whole days on only a handful of words. Didn't somebody once say that real intimacy occurs in silence? I keep learning lessons, and I don't know where to put them. *Reaching Through the Silence: Accompanying a Friend with Cancer.*

On the good days, at first, she could sit up in bed and we would talk while she pretended to eat the soup I gave her. She was engaged to be married twice before she finally made it to the altar. Her eventual mother-in-law gave her a stack of baby clothes as a wedding present. "I tried to make a joke about it, and she said, 'It's not as if you're young.' I was thirty-one."

"How old are you now?"

"Thirty-eight."

She looks fifty. But then, I do, too, and I'm forty-four and healthy as a horse. I'll nurse everybody I know, and I'll outlive them all. My job is to be the one who lasts.

After he comes home one night, I meet him in the kitchen, where we can talk. "Have you made plans about a funeral?"

His face goes white. "What did Laurie say to you?"

"Nothing. What has she said to you?"

"We don't have to think about that yet." It isn't the first time a man has looked at me with hate. I lost my job at Laurie's company because the man in the cube next to mine didn't think the office was a place to chew gum or listen to light classical, even with earbuds. I kept a log of his non-work calls, but in the end no one let me produce it; I came back from a meeting and found a box on my desk with my pictures and MP3 player in it. "We're downsizing," my manager said, though no one was fired but me, the unmarried woman who knits. Laurie didn't call. Much later, when we became Facebook friends, she said she hadn't known, and that might be true.

"Just pay attention," I say. "It won't hurt to think about songs she especially likes. Not hymns. She doesn't like those."

"No," he says. His tone is humble, and I smile at him. He shakes his head. "No."

"He thinks he's strong," I say to Laurie the next day, and she looks at me with surprise.

"No, he doesn't. He always says I'm the strong one."

"Then he wants to look strong."

Laurie shakes her head. "Where do you get this stuff?"

That night she sits up and smiles when he comes home.

He's brought pasta e fagioli from the good Italian place, and she makes a big deal about the rich smell, spangled with basil, as if he'd made it himself. "Why don't you take some of this, Sunny?" It takes me a moment to recognize that she's sending me home. He's sitting on the bed, looking at her with a cocker spaniel's pure adoration.

"Thanks all the same. I don't like beans." I might as well have said that I didn't like carburetors. When Laurie starts to cough, he holds his hand half an inch from her shoulder. Touch her! She's already broken!

"Thank you for everything, Sunny," he says.

I will be back tomorrow. *The Endless Present: A Friend's Slide to Death.* In front of the coat closet, twenty feet from Laurie's room, I slip on my coat and softly hum a bit of the aria that was just on the radio: *il nome mio nessun saprà.* It's the only line I can remember, but it's beautiful when Pavarotti sings it, and I could have worse songs in my head.

Soup (3)

Laurie

Hearing steps in the hall, I straighten my legs under the covers and close my eyes. I am just on the lip of remembering, every cell straining, like the edge of orgasm. In front of the door, the steps stop, then back silently away while my brain reaches in every direction, almost touching the thing I want.

And then falls short again. I spend hours like this, dancing at the brink of a memory that teasingly winds around me. The things I used to know flicker like fireflies, and I clumsily lunge and clutch at them. Probably I am the dog chasing the car; what would I do if I caught it? While my body busies itself with dying, my mind is bright with what it used to know.

I became a good ice-skater once I got my own skates, and could sharpen the blades. They hissed over the ice and I felt dangerous. I never hurt anybody else, but once I sliced my own leg while I was lacing up and needed four stitches. When I was thirteen I broke my ankle, and that was it for skating, though now, if I try, I remember the scrape of metal on ice, and the high laughter of the girls with elaborate hair who wobbled at the side of the rink. The salty grease of the cheese fries. The screechy video game music bouncing over the ice.

In college, I saw a plum tree in bloom, the first time I'd ever seen one. I collapsed at its base and gazed at the blue sky behind the screen of pink blossoms for an hour, straight through my geology quiz on sedimentary rocks. To this day I don't know what breccias are, and I've done just fine.

Except for the nausea, which is almost constant. The doctors told me that antiemetics are good now. I'm lucky, they told me.

The footsteps come back, and I close my eyes again, though the trick won't work twice in a row.

"Don't you want some soup? You need to eat something."

"No."

"Please? For me?"

I open my eyes. "I'm tired of throwing up." Sunny's face is warped into a caregiver's look of concern, as if she's being graded on her performance. "Smile," I say.

"As soon as you agree to soup."

"No deal."

She stumps away, making sure I hear her annoyance. That makes two of us. Left uninterrupted, wobbling on my unsteady raft, I am nearly happy.

Pain keeps me company, patiently gnawing. The pain is a lap-sized creature with rich fur and spiky teeth constantly growing in. The only way the animal can stop its own discomfort is to gnaw. One of us has to hurt, and I see no reason why it shouldn't be me.

"The new drugs do a good job controlling pain. If it ever gets too much for you, we can help," say the doctors. Right now, I'm interested in the creature. It's been a while since I've had a pet, and I like the plush, velvety fur.

I crave, of all things, cheesecake. This is not something to tell Michael, who would bring home four of them when I can't even hold down a soft-boiled egg. But while my brain is ranging amid the glittering memories like a boy with a stick, I imagine thick, sweet cream cheese and imagine that I want it.

When I was a girl, we had a piano made of brown wood. Our kitchen walls were yellow, and my mother washed the white café curtains twice a year. These are not the memories I'm reaching for, though I hold on to the unexpected smell of bleach in the kitchen that lasted a day or so.

A cloud spied through skeletal trees, billowing like whipped cream. A tendril of music, not quite pretty. The smile of the first man I went to bed with. None of these.

During the day it's Sunny in the apartment; at night it's Michael. They try to hide their quarrels from me. The day I married Michael, my shoes pinched. I don't remember the day I met Sunny.

My mother had hatboxes. My sister drowned when I was eight. She had lumpy braids and wore drugstore cologne, and she taught me cat's cradle. There is no reason for that to make me cry.

Sunny must be hovering just outside the door; at the first sniffle she bursts in. "What's wrong? What hurts?"

"Everything."

"Do you want me to call the doctor?" And then, in an unexpected blossoming of something like insight, "Are you afraid?" She leans in, ready to take my fear away. Once, somewhere, I watched water fall over a stone.

I dredge up a smile and paste it crookedly on my face. I've sat at sickbeds, too, and it isn't easy. I should be nicer to her. "If you go away, I'll eat some soup later."

"No, you won't."

For that I give her a real smile. "I'll try."

"You need to fight. You'll win if you just fight." Her broad face is fiercely cheerful, stupid as a cabbage, and my eyes brim again. She doesn't understand a goddamn thing.

I'm still crying when Michael comes home, and I hear the whispers at the front door. Next to my bed, he says, "What changed?"

"Nothing."

Soup (3)

I watch him keep himself from saying, *Sunny said.* We smile at each other, and I wipe snot from my nose.

"Do you want me to sleep next to you tonight?"

"Yes." He wants me to make a choice, so I do. Eventually, after carefully not making any noise, he will drop off to sleep. Then I'll be free to turn my back on him and push my mind harder while my back arcs against the pain that's generally worse at night. Gritty sand on a linoleum floor. The shock of ice against skin. A baby's shriek cutting a room in half. Dizzying, almost sickening honeysuckle.

The slam of a car door. My skating coach's whistle. Library's clean must.

Cold ashes. Cat's sharp whisker. Petals.

Sesame seeds. Gravel. Perfume. Water. Light.

Light.

Song

I overreacted, I admit it. I flew across the kitchen at my eleven-year-old son Nathan, who was playing with my phone and had found his way to "Moondance," and I knocked the phone out of his hand so hard the phone wound up in the living room and Nathan on the floor. I held my boy on my lap for the next half hour, apologizing and crying until his shirt was spotty with my tears.

If Roger hears, he'll be furious, but Roger doesn't have to hear. Nathan won't tell him. By the time Roger comes home from work, Nathan will be singing, and Roger will leave again. Insurance never sleeps, which is Roger's good fortune.

As soon as Nathan finds a song he likes, he memorizes it. As soon as he's memorized it, he sings it, a lot. Nathan sings very, very badly. He doesn't have the ordinary kid's wandery voice that is content to land somewhere in the neighborhood of the right note. He finds profoundly wrong notes, notes so wrong they feel vindictive, and then he reproduces them at unbelievable volume. Once I was walking our dog Sadie and heard him from a block away. I had to drag Sadie into the house, where she hid under the bed like a cartoon dog.

Roger tells me to be patient. He tells me to support our son. Then he leaves the house to go to work, and Nathan stays home and sings with a voice that sounds as if it's peeling sound from melody like skin from a potato.

I think it was *My Fair Lady* two years ago that turned the key in Nathan's lock. I was watching in the family room by myself, happily wrapped in the melodies and gowns and accents of some stage-set London, when I heard a sniffle behind the couch and uncovered my saucer-eyed nine-year-old son. He'd never seen a musical. "They just start singing! Like it's normal!"

"A lot of people are surprised by that." At this point Eliza was fantasizing about killing Professor Higgins, and I patted the couch and told Nathan he could watch with me, but he had to be quiet. The next day he remembered the soundtrack with stunning precision.

"The boy's a genius," Roger said, his voice filled with relief. He was leaving the house in which Nathan, hopping from couch to ottoman, was bellowing about lots of coal making lots of 'eat. Nathan sang the soundtrack nonstop for a week and I thought I could outwait him, but then he discovered Adele and I understood with despair what my future held.

"He's never been so happy," Roger said this morning before kissing me good-bye, before I tackled our son. Nathan was standing at the back window, bouncing back and forth between "Ticket to Ride" and "Rolling in the Deep." "I like the ones where I can get really loud," he told us, his face alight.

Something is not right with Nathan. Nuances elude him, as if his brain is a net designed only to hold big, blunt ideas, and not the quicksilver ones that turn A to A-flat, laughter to complicated laughter. So often Nathan is the last one in the room to finish laughing at a joke. He has been tested and tested and tested—not autism, not Asperger's, simply "on the spectrum," as if the spectrum is a lane where my son has a tidy cottage.

"Try to keep his life stable. That's how he'll do best," the tester told us. Isn't that true of every child?

We tried hard to believe he wasn't special. When he was five years old we said, "He's *five*. Give the kid a chance." Then he was six, eight. Now he's eleven, and Roger's kiss skims off my cheekbone before he leaves the house. If Nathan were suddenly to start singing like Andrea Bocelli, Roger would still need to work early, late, and often. There will not be another child, or even a shared bed. Walk far enough, and you can't retrace steps anymore. There are too many turns, and the path is confused, and the lookouts that were once arresting have turned dun and cold.

These are the thoughts I entertain when Nathan's at school, singing for his classmates and teacher, who sends home a note. These are the thoughts I can have when the house is quiet enough to contain thoughts.

Here is my thought for today: I must find Nathan another song. I cannot bear to hear him sing "Moondance."

John didn't last long. A few months so overheated and hectic and dizzyingly sweet, the memory still makes my heart trip. Roger had someone then, too: hence John. When Roger told me that he had broken things off, he looked at me pointedly until I picked up the phone. Afterward I went to the bathroom and vomited. Roger was in the living room with Nathan. When I came back out, wiping my mouth, he handed our son to me as if Nathan were a toddler, and left the house to go back to work. We were keeping things stable.

John managed the produce department of our Publix. At first we just smiled at each other until one day he handed me a beautiful peach, heavy with juice. Then it was just a matter of time.

"Moondance" happened one afternoon we had sneaked away. We sat in his car and he played the song over and over. To this day the song means gray fabric upholstery and the long burn of bourbon from a flask and low winter afternoon sun directly in my eyes, so I could see nothing but light. He told me he wanted to see me at night. I said, "That can't happen."

"I know. That's why I play this. I imagine you with me, and I cry and hate Roger and hate you. Then I play it again and think about what your shoulder might look like at night. Then sometimes I hit something. Every time I end by thinking about the first time I noticed you, standing in the store looking lost. I wanted to save you. That's when I still thought you'd let me."

A day hasn't passed that I don't remember.

Nathan has finished his cereal. Soon it will be time to leave for school. He asks if he can have my phone back, and penitently, I give it to him. He treats me to Adele and the Beatles and even—auld lang syne—a chorus of "Wouldn't It Be Loverly." "Which one do you like best?" he says.

He's never asked about a playlist before, never seemed to be aware of an audience that existed for any reason except to applaud. No new awareness sparkles from his eyes, but now I'm paying close attention, and watch the way his hand absently opens and closes on the tabletop. I say, "I like the songs with gentle emotions. It's nice to be loud only some of the time."

He wrinkles his face. He's working on it. "Loud is fun."

"I know. But sometimes soft is good, too." This moment is coming too fast. I needed time to prepare, but my son stands before me, his brain's work nearly audible. "Listen," I say, and hit "Moondance," the only song in that moment I can remember whose emotions are soft and good. When it's over Nathan takes the phone from me and plays it again. By the third time he's moving his lips. I dampen mine. "Come on, son. Sing. Let me hear it."

Fat

I'm not fat enough for Big Beautiful Girls sites. The guys who promise to adore a woman's righteous curves are not talking to me. Neither, obviously, are the ones that end their posts with "No Fat Girls ☺" A site for me would say: "I'm looking for something, but I'm not sure what. What's your name again?"

When Em at Reception asks if anyone wants to join her for drinks after work, she is not asking me. The sign-up sheet for the Adopt-a-Highway cleanup weekend rarely gets to my desk. After the Fourth of July party, I stop by Mike in Accounting's cube and compliment him on his home run that saved the game for us, fifth floor always playing against fourth floor.

"Were you there?"

At the end of the day I go home and brush my sister's

hair until it spills down her back in a glassy sheet. We both like this. I haven't told her about Jordan. He's new, and he stopped at my desk before his first week was out. "It's Sherry, right?"

"Sherry-from-HR. Distinct from Sherry-from-Accounting."

"I'll never keep everybody straight." His smile is rueful, blinding, straight out of Hollywood.

"You'll forget there was ever a time you didn't know," I assure him.

"Good to meet you, Sherry-from-HR."

You didn't have to be the fat girl to hear the flirt.

Because I eat lunch at my desk where people can see, a typical meal looks like a poster from a nutritionist's classroom: one pear, one cup of greens with lemon juice, three ounces of poached chicken breast. Often I can't do more than pick at it, since I'm stuffed from the cheesecake I ate in the car on my way to work. It isn't hunger, exactly. Hunger is a friend, a presence I understand. This other thing, this compulsion, has no name. Often it's the opposite of hunger—I eat through indigestion, through fullness, through the rich self-disgust that accompanies me like a choir while I, the fat girl, sing at the front of the stage.

"Get over yourself," says my sister, wincing while I work a knot from her fine hair. Her body slopes out from her neck in a lazy succession of folds. She hasn't been able to fit into a desk chair in years, but she can type from her bed or armchair. She blogs about disability and fat as a political issue, and has posted one photograph of herself, looking tragic and almost boneless, a head floating on top of pools of flesh. Beside her I look stout, capable, and forgettable. My sister's hair looks terrific.

I am not about to tell her about Jordan. She tells me about patriarchy and commodification, and I pay the pizza guy. I may not eat as much as she does, but I eat my share. Before I go to bed, I'll join her for cake. The difference between us is that after I close my bedroom door, I'll do one hundred stomach crunches, because I'm still trying.

I know I won't see Jordan the next day, but I still dress with extra care, my heart rapping out a quick beat that is the rhythm track to every happy love song in the world. For the rest of the week I keep dressing with extra care, and I don't eat anything on the drive to work, so I attack that chicken breast with zeal when lunchtime rolls around. I try not to look too enthusiastic. If there's one thing people notice about the fat girl, it's what she's eating.

My sister has caught on, and is watching every morsel that slips into my mouth. "I don't want to have to take you to the hospital again."

"You never took me to a hospital."

"You were passing out."

"I was fourteen and stupid." I had gone for nine days on nothing but black coffee and sugarless gum. I wouldn't mind having a little of that self-control back again. Now, under my sister's rigid eye, I eat a full serving of mac and cheese.

Fat

My sister eats: the second half of a bag of potato chips. Mac and cheese. Milk. Broccoli gratin that I microwave. Cake, and then ice cream. I hide the idea of Jordan like a locket between my breasts, which I keep strapped in a brassiere as sturdy as a saddle. My sister's breasts spread and puddle like pudding, like heavy gravy. It is so hard to look at her and not think of food.

At work, while Em is asking who wants to go out for drinks at five o'clock, I pore over staff birthdays, because parties are my responsibility. The next birthday is Mike in Sales, two weeks away. I order the cake and one balloon bouquet. Then, from a different site, I order a skirt to have sent to me at work. I know what lines are slimming, and there's plenty of room to change in the bathroom.

Jordan's birthday is six months from now, Leo, a fire sign that would go well with my airy Libra. I know better than to think like this. If I don't stop myself, soon there will be pills in my purse, and phone calls to numbers from HR files that I have access to. Twice I've had to change jobs. My sister says she will stay with me until I understand what I'm doing. I understand perfectly.

This afternoon Jordan waves to me in the parking lot. "Sherry-from-HR!" he calls. "I'm coming to see you soon."

"Jordan-from-New-Accounts! Why are you coming to see me?"

He walks toward me, and the smile makes my eyes fill. He says, "Everybody should have a friend in HR. HR knows the dark secrets."

"Your birthday is in August, and you were at Nicholson and Nicholson before you joined us. Pretty tame secrets, really." He brings home $5,007.43 a month, and hasn't yet started up a 401(k). His marital status is left blank.

"I'll have to up my game. Who gets to judge your secrets?" he says.

"No one in HR has secrets. Company policy."

His hand on my wrist is slightly sunburned, and roughened. I have the clear sense that my beating heart is working its way up my throat. "Can we be friends?" he says.

He's been fired three times in five years. Twice there were questions about bookkeeping and billing, once a complaint. But no accusations ever filed!

"You'll have to fill out some paperwork," I say, the standard HR joke. His squeeze on my wrist is so light I almost don't feel it over my crashing pulse.

I collapse into the driver's seat and need ten minutes before I can start the car. Once home I'll order Indian for dinner; my sister and I have every delivery service on speed dial. I'll brush her hair. She'll talk, and if she thinks I'm not listening, she'll tip something over. "Poor motor control," she says as if it's an accomplishment, and then she'll wait until I come back with the paper towels and bucket before she starts to talk again. This time I'll make her wait.

Pebble

Not yet: The day before Easter, all three kids in the kitchen with five dozen boiled eggs and neat pots of dye, the air stinging with vinegar. No one ever admitted throwing the first egg. The stained wallpaper stayed up until it was time to sell the house.

Not yet: The Easter glorious even without eggs, the boys in their suits handsome and slick, the girl's starched yellow dress as pretty as a tulip, the mother confidently singing "Jesus Christ Is Risen Today" so she could be heard in the last pew. "You are a perfect American family!" a friend says, and the mother smiles because it would be rude to agree. That afternoon the children's grandfather will die of a heart attack in front of them, but not yet.

•

Already: Diphtheria. Scarlet fever. Malaria, malaria, malaria (WWII, Pacific). Disease is behind them, and all they see in front of them is tennis courts and skis. In the evenings, bundled up, they go to the beach. Just after sunset the light that has no source shows them the limitless horizon, and they talk about his day, and her day, and what they will do together the next day.

Not yet: Perfect babies in a row, one, two, three. Their faces are as sweet as blossoms. In a moment of whimsy she won't ever replicate, she finds photographs of roses and pastes her babies' faces at the centers.

Now: Even though they are almost married, they are shy when they look at each other. Too much happiness is unsafe. They would not claim to be beautiful, but they are tall and handsome, and the bad things are behind them. They know there is no reason they should be unreasonably happy, but they don't see any reason they shouldn't.

Or rather: Happiness is waiting to be picked up, like the smooth pebbles on the beach. He finds one to skip, but it sinks on the first try. He laughs and picks up another. The beach is full of them.

Silly. You don't *say* these things.

Not yet: The big ski trip, the one they are all looking forward to. He grumbles about the cost every chance he gets, pretending not to be proud. Their daughter drinks the good Swiss chocolate, happy for once. Thirteen is not a happy year. Tickled to see her smiling, they let her follow her hotdogging brothers to the top of the black diamond run. Her brothers promise they'll take care of her, and no one has the heart to blame them when she falls, twisting, obliterating her left knee. They should be blamed. She loses the leg.

Not yet: One hospital after another. She cries through her PT, refuses to do her exercises at home, spits at the therapist. She gets fat. Pills, pills, pills, pills, pills.

Not yet: The kindergarten-aged daughter brings her mother a bouquet from the backyard, even the stout geraniums wilting from the heat of the little girl's grip. The mother thanks her, and then thanks her again because the girl continues to stand in front of her. Finally her daughter says, "Don't I get a cookie?"

Not yet: The dinner out, just the two of them. It took months to plan, and she thinks up topics for conversation. She is determined not to talk about the kids, and so is he. Picking up his wineglass—it really is a night on the town—he says, "To our happiness." "Don't," she says. "It's true," he says. "*Don't say it.*"

Already: The hungry days, the making do. Shirts made out of dresses made out of uniforms. The magazine pictures of movie stars on the walls. When he proposes, he promises her real china, a yard with flowers, children one, two, three. A butterfly bobs next to them, grazing her shoulder, and they laugh. She rests her face next to his and bats her eyelashes against his cheek, a butterfly kiss.

Not yet: Are they boyfriends? The father calls them thugs, which is better than what the mother is thinking: *pimps.* Their daughter's eyes are walls. After one night out, she comes in without her prosthesis. The next morning she says she lost it, and by noon she says she broke it. The whole family has learned that needle marks don't only show up in arms, and they try to think of ways that they could casually glance between her toes.

Not yet: "Stop teasing your sister." "We don't use that kind of language." "Stop teasing your sister." "WHO left this in the bathroom?" "Stop teasing your sister." "Stop talking. Just. Stop. Talking."

Not yet: Laughter from upstairs so shrill it's like a fire alarm, and then a scream. They can ignore the noise, but when silence falls they race up the stairs to find all three kids, panting, pajamas stuck to their sweat, and the bed slumped where they'd been jumping. The long silence stretches with the children's eyes fearfully tracking their parents. "Oops," says the oldest boy.

At his daughter's funeral, the father collapses. "I can't sit at the front," he whimpers. The aisle is dominated by the casket, closed. There was only so much the mortician could do with the blue-black face, the tongue like a sausage. The mother's face goes rigid. In the end, she sits with her sons in the front pew while her husband sobs at the back of the church, facedown on the carpet.

•

Now: She is much better at this than he is. She finds a good, flat rock, and with a whip of her wrist sends it skipping over the placid surf: three, four, five. "Beat that," she says, her face shining.

"I can't," he says, admiring her unruly hair, "but I'll tell you this—"

She slaps her hand, salty, over his mouth. "Not one more word."

"Or what?" He grins. She is a fine-looking woman.

She picks up another pebble. Just as she lets it go, the sun slips away from a scrap of cloud and dazzles the crinkled water. No telling how far that rock goes before it slides under the water.

Pariah

Of all the scenarios I imagined, this one never came up: my heart leaping at the sight of Iris Murphy. She takes ten minutes to cross the post office lobby so she can stand in line, where she complains about how federal employees— "That's the same as *my* employees, you know"—take too long to weigh her letters. She smells bad, but she meets my eye when she finally gets to the counter, and doesn't pretend to be looking at stamps until she can get another teller. I say, "How are you, Iris? How is your cat?"

In a small town, news and gossip break first in front of the out-of-town mail slot. The day Marie McIlvoy's son found out he passed the bar, I went into the back and broke out some Franzia we had left over from a birthday party, about as against the law as you want. The wine was awful, but we all felt like we were getting away with something,

189

which is fine, it turns out, until you try to get away with the wrong thing.

Back two years, when I used to be married, my ex Cindy worked at the hospital. She called from work to tell me things, like when Henry Lipert had been admitted for a heart attack, so I could put a hold on his mail without anybody asking. It was good to be able to do small things to help people, and Cindy and I were famous for helping people. We reached out, we volunteered. We were nice.

Two nice people can share a house for a long time. They can have nice meals and nice sex. It isn't a bad life, animated by nice conversations about the people you know. Standing side by side with your spouse, looking out onto your nice life, the view is comfortable. Then one of you looks off to the side, and everything goes to hell.

Robin wasn't as pretty as Cindy. Several people have told me so. She also wasn't as kind. "What are you *thinking?*" Marie Bledsoe snarled, the last thing she said to me. Her husband, Terry, explained that if there were another post office, they'd go there. I knew I'd lose some friends. I just didn't think I'd lose all of them.

Robin and I didn't even last a year. Not as pretty, not as kind. Unwilling to overlook the sounds I apparently make when I chew, which Cindy brought up, too, in our short-lived mediation when I was trying to get her to take me back.

Robin had just been another customer, once a month with the postage meter, little jokes about the crap picture of Elvis on the commemorative stamp, until one day she said, "This is my third time here in two days. I wanted to get you to wait on me." Right there in front of everybody. She was wearing a brown sweater, and the hair that curled back from her face was touched with red, and I couldn't tell you how long it had been since I had noticed anything.

After that it was nothing but noticing: Cindy's stained panties in the laundry; the rush of breath behind Robin's words, almost a lisp, sexy; the treacherous, dove-colored skim of ice in front of the post office door. I stared at it until my supervisor made me go out and spread rock salt. Iris had almost fallen.

For two months Robin and I were blazing, as constant as teenagers, in our cars, outside in the lake park where we melted the snow, in motels where it wasn't as exciting, with sheets and bedside tables and lamps, as it was in the tiny back seat of her car where our hot breath made her hair curl more. I came home shaking as if I had a fever, and Cindy asked if I wanted a cup of coffee. I was forty-eight years old and looking at the rest of my life.

When I ran into Ron McClurg a month ago, he walked right past me, even though I said his name. It took me a while to realize that I was being snubbed. I didn't know the rules.

People want me to leave town, and I'd like to accommodate them, but what would I leave *to*? The only software I know belongs to the USPS. I can do some good here—whenever anybody at work needs to trade a shift, they come to me. "I'm our utility infielder," I offered when Denise asked me to switch shifts.

"Is that a joke?" she said.

"No," I said, which was the same as saying "Yes" or "*No habla inglés*," since she'd already turned away, leaving me to greet Iris, waiting with a flat parcel that I would privately readdress to cover her shaky handwriting.

"Guess you're stuck with me," she said.

"We're always happy to see you, Iris," I said.

"Don't add lying to your list of sins." Smelling like old tea, she wore one pilled gray sweater over another pilled gray sweater and moved as if her knees had rusted shut. A nice person would have felt sorry for her.

"I hope there's not a list," I said.

"There's a list." She handed me her parcel. "Be careful with this. It's my parents' wedding picture. I don't want it bent."

I made myself smile, not reminding her that she could have packed it in cardboard to protect it. Ringing up the postage, I said, "How's your cat?"

At first I didn't notice her silence. Not until I looked up from the keypad did I see her glaring at me. "I don't have a cat. I've never had a cat. *Not every old woman has a cat.*"

Reflexively I looked around, ready to be embarrassed, but Denise was already gone, and there were no other customers.

"How's your girlfriend?" Iris said.

"Same as your cat," I said.

"I doubt it. My cat likes me."

Iris paid in cash, the last two dollars in coins. After the door closed behind her, I took her package, slipped it into a sturdy box and wrote the address legibly. I used cat stamps for the postage. Those were all the things I was supposed to do. Next I did the thing I wanted: cracking the box hard across my knee, stamping it FRAGILE, and dumping it in the outgoing mail. There was a box there from Ron McClurg, too, and I picked it up and shook it. Nothing broken yet.

Priest

When Father Tom comes to a party, people look embarrassed, even the ones who invited him. It's the collar. At wedding and funeral receptions, he is seated at the table with the great-aunts. He is the necessary conduit, but he frightens people who hear "priest" and imagine no house, no family, no sex. "You must have started so young!" a parishioner recently said to him. "I'm always surprised when young men—"

She faltered, and Father Tom was moved to pity. "Me, too," he said.

He didn't start especially young. He went to college, got a job as a loan officer, and tried to understand the misery that swept over him every morning when he cinched up his tie. He had a girlfriend and met his car payments. There was no reason for him to find himself standing in his apartment garage with a rope and instructions he'd downloaded for tying a noose.

"I'm glad you didn't follow through," said the priest Tom talked to later, because a priest was cheaper than a therapist.

"Bad at knots," Tom said.

The priest thought Tom's answer was God, of course, and Tom forgave him for that. It was the priest's job to think that despair at life's unsolvable monotony could be solved by God, and it was Tom's job to listen politely, go home, and get any ropes or extension cords out of the house.

He was back at the church a week later. "Give me something to do," Tom said, and the priest handed him a rake. Three hours later, when he had sweated through his flannel shirt and streaked his face with leaf dirt, he felt better than he had felt in months. "What else do you have?" he asked the priest, who told him to come back after he'd had a shower.

He tutored kids in math and washed forks after the parish potluck. He vacuumed the sacristy. He braced himself for the inevitable next talk about God, which came like clockwork. "How can you be so sure you're not priest material?" the priest said.

"I'm not sure I believe in God," Tom said.

"You don't have to be sure about God. You just have to believe in God's work," the priest said, words that Tom could not resist. The work—God's work, whatever—was everywhere, the world bleeding from every orifice. "How can you stand it?" his girlfriend asked after he spent a weekend locked in with violent offenders.

"They're people, too," he said lamely, unable to meet her sad eyes. Tom and his girlfriend hadn't had sex in weeks, hadn't been out to dinner in months, but he kept volunteering for the lock-ins. He felt coherent with the killers and freaks. When he moved toward ordination and one examiner after another asked him whether he was sure he had a vocation, he told them, "I don't think any-one can be sure. But I feel close to myself when I'm doing this work." Once upon a time, the examiners would have pressed him about whether he felt close to God, but no one talked like that anymore.

But now, now that the vows are finished and the rest of his life is signed away and set out to collect dust, he's tired of being close to himself. At the end of the day, af-ter the meetings are finished and the computer shut off, the unanswerable questions return. When his mother was close to death, she caught at his sleeve and pulled until his ear was next to her mouth. "I'm afraid," she whispered.

"It's okay."

"I'm not supposed to be afraid. It means I don't have faith."

"Mom, everybody—"

She shook her head. "I'm going to go to hell."

He almost laughed. "Trust me. You're not."

She turned her face from him and died two days later,

and nothing the mortician did could erase the terror from her face.

He prays for her, of course. But there isn't enough prayer in the world. Not for his mother, not for the hemophiliac girl he knew in grade school who got knocked down and bled out on the playground, not for continents full of children waking up with a stomach full of hungry and no food for miles. No one has answers, his confessor has told him. Is that supposed to make Father Tom feel better?

One night, maddened by his circling, ceaseless thoughts, he dropped to the worn carpet and forced himself through push-ups until his arms gave out. He hadn't done push-ups since he was in high school, and his arms burned after twenty, but at least he quit thinking about the argument he'd had with his mother the night before he started college, the one that left her weeping in the bathroom after he told her that heaven was a fairy tale. In the morning he made himself pray the Daily Office, which he skipped so often he hardly remembered how to do it.

The trick is to drive away thoughts. No wonder the ancients believed in demons; as far as Father Tom can see, demonic possession is a perfectly reasonable way to interpret the memories that assail him. "Do you have trouble not thinking about sex?" his confessor asks in a confiding tone. Sex is the least of it. Father Tom remembers his girlfriend's face, scrubbed of emotion, when he told her he was going to become a priest. "So I get dumped for Jesus," she said.

Sometimes he prays, sometimes he does squats or jumping jacks, one week he drank a glass of water every half hour, peed like a racehorse, and lost two pounds. These actions—mortifications, to use the old word— make him a better priest, a better person. If he'd discovered discipline a little sooner, he wouldn't have made his mother cry and might never have entered the priesthood. Wearing his belt one notch too tight, he counseled a gay fourteen-year-old for three straight hours. The boy was cutting himself; he showed Father Tom the neat scars laddering up his leg. Father Tom leaned back in his chair, feeling the belt sawing at his soft waist. "What would happen?" he said. "What would happen if you never cut yourself again? What if you made peace with the dryness in your heart?" The boy is in college now, and his mother thinks he's happy.

A few weeks after that counseling session, Father Tom holds a blade against his thigh, bouncing it lightly. The razor blade makes a light pinging sensation on his skin; it's keen and unexpectedly lighthearted. Father Tom is teasing himself; nothing will come of this. He has too much work to do. Just a week ago he agreed to spearhead a new outreach to troubled youth downtown, an agreement he made while knuckling a finger backward painfully under the desk. "I'm so glad," said the social worker who had called the meeting, a brisk woman with a terrible haircut. "No one reaches people better than you do. Sometimes I think, when I look at you, that I'm seeing the face of Jesus."

"Jesus is either horrified or laughing himself sick," Father Tom said.

"You need to learn to accept a compliment, Father."

"Thank you," he said, forcing his finger back a millimeter further. The woman meant to be kind, and he was not ungrateful. She had no way to understand that Father Tom and Jesus have worked out their own understanding. In the meantime, he will practice the little deaths, every day. Death, which Jesus treated so cavalierly, will eventually come to save Father Tom. It is a life. It makes him happy.

Artist

After a long shoot my shoulders and back ache, and if anybody can tell me about a bar nearby, I head straight over. The faceys don't go because they've already had their eight hundred calories for the day, but the hand model is allowed to drink a beer. "Just don't let my fingers get cut," I tell the bartenders, who open bottles for me. Sometimes, if I've been there for a while, I copy the old frat-boy trick and open the bottle with my teeth. Nobody cares about my teeth.

Today's shoot was Mop Up paper towels. All day long I snaked my arm around the refreshed roll of Mop Ups so that the camera saw a youthful hand effortlessly ripping off a single perfect towel. Claudio, the photographer who says he's an artist, noted every time I missed my mark. "To the left. Make it light," he said. "No veins." My fingers light as wind, I ripped towel after towel, careful to keep my shadow out of the shot. "Too far. No veins!"

You would drink, too. I'll bet Claudio did, off at an important bar with the water-drinking faceys. He was explaining to them how he's an artist, and they were nodding, because they were his art.

Officially my title is parts model. Some girls don't just do hands, but feet, too, or even legs. My only part is hands. I watch TV clumsily, hands dipped in lanolin and covered by heavy latex mittens, and scrutinize other hands peeling a banana or wiping a window. Don't for one second imagine this isn't a serious business. There are new hands, young ones, coming along every day.

In my other life I'm a temp. "No cooking jobs," I say, and ideally no typing jobs, either. I can't afford anything that might nick my nail polish or make my hands look muscular; the ideal hand model's hands are as free of definition as pooled cream, like the hands of a Chinese concubine.

"And you know about Chinese concubines how?" says Greg. He was waiting for me at the bar tonight, though we hadn't made any plans. He's my favorite photographer, joking through every shoot and working at a speed that a mortal can keep up with. Back when we were together— not long—we joked that we were the power couple of parts modeling.

"Saw a TV show."

"You watch too much TV."

"It's how I do my homework." I pluck one napkin from the dispenser, making sure to display its snowiness. The napkin is the star. Then I pick up my martini glass so that he can see the slight tilt at the end of my thumb. That thumb and the narrow back of my hand are my big assets. They separate me from the girls who think that straight fingers and deep nail beds are enough.

"You sure you need that?" Greg says.

"A photographer is criticizing somebody else's drinking?"

"You've got a shoot tomorrow."

He's looking at the tabletop, not me. We both know that it doesn't matter if I come to a shoot with bloodshot eyes, as long as I can hold a candle or tomato or bottle of furniture polish with rock-steady hands. "What have you heard?"

"Claudio is bitching."

"Claudio is a bitch."

Greg's voice sinks. "On the last job? With the facey?"

It was a moisturizer spot, and I was the hands. Those jobs are murder: I crouch behind the facey and guess where her chin is, her throat, her mouth. Even on my best days there are some misses, and a few times makeup had to come and completely redo her. No matter what you think, I never meant to smear her lipstick. "There's no hand model in the world who doesn't sometimes miss."

"Claudio says there are a lot. He says he's not going to work with you anymore. He wants you off the shoot."

"It's a goddamn paper-towel spot. Artist, my ass."

"It's work. Do you have anything else lined up?"

I looked at my martini, mystifyingly half empty. What I had lined up was two weeks filling in for a receptionist at a gypsum company. I did not know what gypsum was.

"Claudio's a loudmouth," Greg said. "Don't give him anything to talk about. You can get your career back on track." He patted my shoulder before he left.

Who has a career as a parts model? Kimbra Hickey. Her pallid hands hold the luridly red apple on the cover of *Twilight*, the book on millions of shelves in America. She goes to *Twilight* conferences where she takes pictures with her fans. Now that she's famous, people want to see her face. She re-creates the *Twilight* pose with apples that fans provide and signs a few autographs, though not enough to endanger her hands' sweet, untested look.

Kimbra Hickey can afford to have someone sign books for her, open bottles for her, drive cars and pick cherries and play the violin for her. "I'm in a bar now so I don't have to make my own martini," I say to the air. The bartender and I share a moment's gaze that could mean anything. If I'd been a facey, he would have gotten my phone number.

Instead, I go home. On the table next to my front door is a tub of industrial-strength moisturizer that I put on immediately; it makes my hands slippery, but it smooths them out like nothing else. Then I go to the refrigerator where a half-full bottle of sauvignon blanc needs to be drunk tonight if it's going to be any good. I'm doing fine, I'm perfectly stable, I can handle two martinis, and then the bottle slips and I dive for it and I'm on the floor with shards of wine bottle all around me, including the one slicing into the meat of my right hand, the hand that holds things. In an instant I'm holding a palmful of blood. Thick blood furling over sheet-white hands: it's what Kimbra Hickey was suggesting with that apple. A photographer should be here.

This is such a good idea that I get up to call Greg. He doesn't live far away, and now, in my kitchen, I've got the image that could make my career. But when I pick up my phone I realize that I have my own camera. It isn't easy, holding the blood-slick phone with my left hand, but I can look at my perfect right hand, a lotus, red at the center. I see exactly how it needs to be. By tomorrow there will be a scar, and I will have to learn about gypsum. Now I manipulate the petals that are my fingers. They throb like strobe lights. This is art. I take the picture.

Parable

Letting Joyce play the organ is an act of Christian charity. She comes every night at five, and her knotted fingers
collapse from one wrong key into another while she holds
the same pedal down for measure after measure until the
sound is nothing but collision. We can hear it from the
office, where productivity goes way up around four thirty.

The arrangement has worked fine, even though my assistant rector Michelle is champing at the bit to have a se-
curity system installed so Joyce would have to code herself
in, a system Joyce couldn't possibly remember. Michelle
reminds us that there are microphones in the church, and
sometimes the kids leave guitars. "Somebody could steal
us blind." No one's done it yet, and if Michelle wants to
take Joyce's key away, she can do it herself.

Joyce is old, she's lonely, she's unwashed. Yesterday she

caught me in my office when I was trying to find one new thing to say about the parable of the talents. She cleared her throat and asked if I was busy, and I answered with the kind of heartiness that makes children cry. Come in! Come in!

She shuffled in the door, managing to make her loafers sound like house slippers. Her head was sunk between her shoulders, and her face was almost maroon. At first I thought she was having a heart attack, but the poor woman was blushing.

"I need to tell you something."

"That's good, Joyce. That's what I'm here for. Sit down, please."

"Something happened to me. While I was playing the organ."

"Did somebody say anything to you? Did somebody break in?"

She snorted grimly. "My playing doesn't exactly attract people."

"No one wants to disturb you," I said lamely.

"You're kind to give me time. But it's your job to be kind."

"Won't you sit down, Joyce?"

"I—." Both frightened and hostile, she was a starving dog protecting its single, stripped-bare bone. She stared at me with eyes so round and red they looked boiled, then turned and left the office before I could stop her, her loafers *shff, shff, shff* down the hall. The woman is eighty-four, and she's been coming to this church for sixty-five years. She's been widowed as long as I've known her, but I don't know whether she has children, or where she grew up. I stared at the spot where she'd stood and let shame coat the inside of my mouth. Tonight, a little past five, I went into the church.

Joyce was playing what she has always played: an unwavering 4/4 rhythm, straight-up third-fifth chords, music like cinderblocks. She went through five mind-numbing verses of "The King of Love My Shepherd Is" without so much as a grace note's variation. By the time she stopped, my shoulders were up to my ears. I called out, "Can we go back to our conversation?"

After a long pause, she said, "It isn't a conversation. It's a confession."

I said, "It can't be that bad, Joyce," a little more honest than I should have been.

She waited me out, staying at the keyboard until I made my way to her, and she looked down at me from the organ bench. She said, "I used to try to do the things real organists do, but I just sounded stupid, so I do what I know how to do. I play the hymns. Please don't think I'm putting on airs."

"No one would think that."

After a full minute, she said, "The other night, about a week ago, I heard a noise while I was playing. I stopped, but I didn't see anybody. Then I started playing again, and I heard a creak, as if a door was opening or somebody sitting in a pew. When it was no one the second time, I knew my ears were playing tricks on me. So I kept playing. I sang, too." She swallowed. She sings like the old woman she is, one long quaver.

"How strange," I said.

"Please just listen. I finished the last verse, the noise was a lot louder, and I looked beyond the lectern. The sanctuary was full of *people*. *People* were here, hundreds of them, taking up the pews and the aisles. They were talking to each other and nodding, waiting for the service to start. They looked happy to be here. I was not taking drugs."

"I know you weren't, Joyce."

Tears crowded her voice. "This is what I saw. They all were coming to church, so many people. I couldn't play well enough for them. They needed someone good, and what they had was me." She tucked her hands under her thighs.

"You were exactly good enough," I said, the words I was supposed to say. "You were what brought them. They wanted you."

"That is not possible," she said.

I put my hand on Joyce's knee, pants that probably haven't been washed in a month, and felt the alarming warmth of skin beneath. "You understand what happened, don't you? You were rewarded for giving what you have in worship. You were given a vision."

"I am crazy," she said. "And you're seeing it."

"You are blessed."

Parable

"So blessed that you want me to play on Sunday?"

It took a while for her to go home, tears still rimming her eyelids. After I hear her car leave the parking lot I walk away from the organ, an instrument I don't think Joyce will want to touch again, and go back into the worship space. No noise troubles me other than my firm footsteps on the rug. I sit for a while in one of the pews, looking toward the lectern where I usually stand, but nothing feels strange. I won't tell anyone about Joyce. She wants her vision to be a secret, and so do I.

Easing out of the pew, I press my cheek to the cool wall. I have never seen hundreds of people in this church. One Christmas, we got ninety-seven envelopes in the collection basket, our all-time high. I have done my best to be sincere, and to give voice to God. I have given this my life.

The plaster under my cheek has grown warm. I turn back to face the empty church, clear my throat, and say, "'For it will be like a man going on a journey, who called his servants and entrusted to them his property. To one he gave five talents, to another two, to another one, to each according to his ability.'" The words fall to the floor. I can preach all night if I want to.

"Who among us hasn't wanted to be given five talents? We know all about one talent, or even two. Who gets five? I'd like to meet that person. I'd like to know what it feels like."

Happiness

When her daughter is finished trying on clothes, Mrs. Bryant watches the young woman head out to the parking lot, then comes back to the dressing room and tries on every piece her daughter just discarded. She judges her arms in the silk tank, her butt in the Japanese denim jeans, alert for sag or pull or dimpling. I make no comment when she cries. She's probably forty-five, could pass for thirty-five, wants to be twenty-five.

The other sales clerks circle Mrs. Bryant, who is blood in the water. One day, when I wasn't working, another clerk sold her $2,000 worth of denim she will never, ever wear. "We're not running a charity here," said the other clerk. Not at Barneys prices, we're not.

Mrs. Bryant's hair shines like ice over her shoulders. Her bras and panties match; when Mr. Bryant undresses her he finds a lovely little package. The wallet inside her handbag costs as much as my monthly rent. These are not reasons to hate her. When she comes into the store she looks as dazzled and lost as a child. This isn't a reason to hate her, either.

I'm not normally a nice person. Once I sold a girl a pair of $1,800 Manolos that were a full size too small; she was already limping when she posed in front of the mirror. "Look at how they lengthen your legs!" I said.

A customer looks at a pair of shoes and thinks about the night they would mean—the party they promise, the pictures, the life. I help her see that life, and then I embellish it, because it's my job to see more than she does, and to increase her joy.

Mrs. Bryant doesn't see a new life. She drags in her daughter, who flees after half an hour. Her daughter started college, then stopped, and now has started again. "I don't know what she wants," Mrs. Bryant says. Her daughter's first major was something like economics, or maybe computers. The new major at the new college is foreign relations, which Mrs. Bryant can remember because her daughter keeps bringing foreigners home.

"I'm not very smart," Mrs. Bryant confides. "So I have to look good."

"You're right," I said. She's already trying to see the future, making plans. That makes her smarter than most of our clients, who can't imagine seeing past tomorrow.

Mrs. Bryant doesn't know my name. After all this

time, this embarrasses her. Every once in a while she takes a stab, murmuring *Linda* or *Sharon*. It's Emma.

Yesterday, while admiring her in a cocktail dress with a back so low the fabric looked as if it would slip right off in a shining puddle, I said, "I have breast cancer."

"This would be a good dress for you to wear. No one would be looking at your front."

"But I don't go anywhere I could wear that dress."

"Wear it to work," she said. She left without buying anything, but she'll be back. I haven't worked here for seventeen years for nothing.

None of the other sales clerks know that I'm sick. Treatments will start soon. I've bought a wig and told my oncologist that the most important thing is suppressing nausea. "I can't go darting out of the dressing room during a fitting," I said.

"You can't expect to keep working," she said. "Soon the fatigue will just be too great. You need to make plans."

"You're a size 6, aren't you? But such a lovely, long torso. You should come in. I have a blouse that will look like it was made for you."

"You're trying to change the subject."

"Do you want me to hold the blouse for you?"

A different sales clerk would have flattered her and called her a 4, but my way is better. Soon she will trust me, and then she will stop talking about me not going to work, where I can find clothes for her and hide them from the other clerks.

I'll be able to lie down when I get home. There's no one in my apartment who needs anything. The husband left when I told him to, with a minimum of fuss. The boyfriend proved stickier. He liked having an apartment with clean windows.

"No kids? Really?" We met at a cocktail party, which I thought meant that he often went to cocktail parties. I was still young, and dumber than Mrs. Bryant. I didn't know that he was an electrician, a project of the hostess, and when I did find out, an electrician seemed exotic. He was handsome, of course. Projects are.

"Is that strange?"

"Don't you want some of you to be in the world after you die?"

"I think the world has all of me it needs."

Later he would agree, but first we had to get through the bagels in bed, and then the brittle texts, and then the money. "It's easy for you," he said. "You don't have children."

I had clean windows and a stocked refrigerator. A drawerful of plunging, painful bras that I bought thinking of him. Soon they will be useless.

"Do you have someone you can rely on, who will get groceries for you on days you can't get them for yourself?" the doctor asked.

"Of course."

"I'll need the phone number," she said.

I gave her Mrs. Bryant's number, the only one I have

memorized. I call it twice a week with news of sales and new shipments. "Just ignore any calls from the hospital," I'll say, and she will.

She's coming to the store this afternoon. I've brought rolling racks into the dressing room and arranged clothes as she does in her own closet, white to black, spring to winter. The clothes are youthful and for three hours I will have to think of nothing more than how they rest against her lovely skin.

Before she can touch a single blouse I will ask, "Would you care for a beverage?" This is what happiness is. I create it.

Dogs

Rain makes the job harder. Roxie, the big Newf mix, would happily walk in a hurricane, but nervous Jackson won't even let me put his collar on if there's thunder within fifty miles. Every dog that gets wet has to be washed, meaning that I come home smelling like dog shampoo, a point Mom makes. She had different hopes for my life.

We used to fight—when high school didn't work out, and then college. The office-skills training course. The paralegal training, the medical assistant's degree, the New Attitudes section at Macy's. "Is it drugs? Is that the problem?" she said. "No," I said, which wasn't quite a lie. I would have flunked all of her intended careers no matter what, though I admit the weed helped. She looked at me and saw potential, which is a mother's right. I looked at myself and saw a train that had already arrived at its station.

Every day has a specific order, to accommodate the owners' schedules and the dogs' needs. Within those stipulations, though, I have a little leeway, and I make sure my workday ends with Hairy and Chester. Hairy and I have been working on a new trick; I say, "*Who's* Hairy?" and he rockets into my arms. At fifty pounds, he's a substantial rocket, and more than once I've landed on my ass, the ecstatic dog licking my face. It's like being licked by a mop. We both love it.

If I like a dog, we work on tricks. The owner doesn't need to know. Everybody wants me to spend time with their dog, not just blast through a ten-minute walk; part of the exclusiveness of my service is the guarantee that I'll spend at least half an hour with every dog—no TV, no texting. I've taught dogs to walk on their hind legs, to clap their paws when the doorbell rings, to sit every time the refrigerator door opens. I taught Otis, a seventeen-year-old shepherd with glaucoma and hips that had turned to concrete, to wag every time I said his name. When he died, I cried all weekend.

"Sometimes animal trainers go to Hollywood. They work on movies and TV shows," Mom said.

"I walk dogs. Nobody in Hollywood is going to care about that."

"You could try. Ambition doesn't cost anything."

Ha.

I used to draw. It was the one thing I was good at in high school, and the only class I could stay awake in. As soon as the teacher started talking, I was nodding along. Shape, line, negative space—I *got* it. At lunch I stayed in the art room, still drawing, still silk-screening, still doing whatever we were doing. The first teacher, Mrs. Ramos, told me I was good. The second one, Mr. Lennox, told me to enter a contest. "I'm not going to do it for you," he said. "But this is where you belong." So I sent six sketches to a statewide competition that would have given me a scholarship. Looking back, I wonder what I would have done with it, but the question didn't come up. The sketches came back crumpled; someone had scrawled "Promising?" at the bottom of one.

"*Who's* Hairy?" Boom.

Chester is amiable and lazy, and has no interest in learning to sing on command or vault over the sofa. Neither does Duke, the fat papillon who still hasn't, at age five, figured out the rudiments of saving his pee for outside. The dogs who are fun to train are the ones who know the sound of my car after they've heard it twice. They lie down and wait when my phone rings. As soon as they learn a trick, they start embellishing it, like the Doberman who bounced on the end of the diving board to get extra height, then turned around in midair before he hit the pool. He had to do it three times before I understood that he was showing off.

I would tell my mother about that Doberman, but the story would make her sad. Sad is where she has lived since her stroke. Her speech is still the same, but she can't walk anymore, or lift her hand high enough to comb her hair.

I do it for her, every morning and often at night, too. She says, "Do you think there's a God?"

"I don't know, Mom."

"I do. And he hates me."

I keep combing. Maybe if Dad was still home, he could have found a way to soothe her, but he ran off years ago, when people at his church found out about the secretary and the missing money and the mission he wasn't really funding in Uganda after all. Mom called that his pastoral trifecta.

Once, after he and Mom quarreled, he took me for a walk—nowhere in particular, just walking to be walking. We walked so far that my legs gave out, and he carried me home. I relived that memory until I wore it out, but sometimes it still comes back to me, his heavy hands gripping my legs. If I knew where he was, I would fly to him.

Mom knows that. Every once in a while she says, "When your father was still in Florida"—or the Caribbean, or Brazil. He bilks other parishes in her stories, and fathers other children. That might all be true. She tells me these stories with an expression of sorrow, but the stroke left her face twisted.

I do my best with her, though I can't make her hair as pretty as it used to be, and she prefers Meals on Wheels food to mine. Once I was helping her out of the tub and she pushed my face away from hers. "You smell," she said. "I'm glad your father isn't here to see this." No telling which of us she was talking about.

I help her with physical therapy in the evenings. The doctor is still hopeful that Mom might regain a little bit of movement, but only with exercise, which Mom hates. I stand beside her bed and say, "Lift your arm just a little, Mom. Just an inch."

"Why?"

That's a stumper. She's never going to be able to comb her hair. She can eat only by dropping her mouth to the edge of the plate and pushing food in, which she prefers to being fed. "You must love this. I eat like a dog," she said last night. I didn't tell her that I loved her, because she didn't want to hear it.

Instead I said, "Just an inch." When she managed it, I didn't tell her how well she was doing or praise her progress. I know how training works. I said, "More."

Job

After the last show, when the passengers demand "Shout" like they always do, Raoul comes to his cabin next to mine and listens to "Giant Steps" eight times in a row. He's a kid, and he still thinks he'll have a life that will let him play Coltrane.

Cruise musicians are supposed to be kids, and this job is great for them. They learn ten words in ten different languages, and they get to try out sex in every port. For a horn player with fresh ink on his music B.A., a cruise-ship gig is a step into the land of professionals. For a sixty-two-year-old guitarist perched on a stool in the Cool Brews Lounge singing "Fire and Rain," every day is ground glass in the soul.

I knew roadies for the Eagles. I knew *J. D. Souther.*

There's a girl on this cruise who comes to hear me every

night. It's been a while since once of these. She looks like she's sixteen, and I'm waiting for her father to introduce himself. The first few days, when we were out of Piraeus and heading for the islands, she just listened. Now she knows my set list and asks for "Fire and Rain" or "Take It Easy" night after night. The songs her parents listened to. Grandparents. She has light brown hair long enough to sit on and big, cowlike eyes. When I play "Yesterday" before my second break, she smiles at me as if we're in on a joke together. All I can think of is banging her until the whole ship rattles, which is why I make sure we never spend one second together that isn't in the company of fifty people.

"Where did you grow up?" she asks. The bartender will serve anybody out of diapers, so she's drinking a margarita. I'm drinking a Coke.

"California." I smile but resolutely do not ask where she's still growing up. This is not a friendship.

"How long have you been playing on ships?"

"Since before you were born."

She dips a finger into her margarita and rubs the salty rim of her glass. "You don't need to be afraid of me."

"Yes, I do," I say, and she smiles.

Her favorite song is "Suite: Judy Blue Eyes," which cannot be played by a solo guitarist. By Mykonos, our fourth night out, I've written an arrangement that I can limp through, and she rewards me with a smile that throbs through my whole body. She brings me a little straw pelican from her shore excursion, and for one night I put it on my dresser. The next morning I brush it into the trash can, where it belongs.

I haven't asked her anything about herself, but I know a few things: She knows a lot about flowers and enjoys looking at Mediterranean hillsides. She likes goats. After I play "Tequila Sunrise," she orders one. "I'd forgotten about these," she says, and I remember drinking them night after night in Topanga Canyon with Linda Rondstadt, who talked about Mexican music that I thought was stupid. Without my asking, the bartender brings me another Coke. The cruise still has six nights to go.

Things I do not know: What her father looks like. Whether there's a boyfriend back home. Where her cabin is. Mine is as far below decks as you can get without actually being on the rope deck, and I share it with the ninety-pound drummer who hates me because I get out of the ship band's eight o'clock Hooray for Hollywood show to play on my stool in Cool Brews. Corinne—her name is Corinne—went to the show with her parents, then slipped out and came to hear the end of my set. I was furious because my heart jumped to see her.

Rhodes, then Patmos, Santorini, and over toward Italy. We end with two nights in Venice, including the only night excursion, to the Lido. The whole cruise leads up to that night, where everybody dresses up and pretends they know how to play baccarat. Passengers come back on the ship with bow ties undone and hair falling down, drowning in sex smell. The bands in the Lido play real music, for people who know how to listen. I tried for years to get a Lido gig.

"Are you going?" Corinne asks. Her foot's been tapping my ankle for the last half hour. At first I kept moving my leg.

"Are you?"

"I have until tomorrow to sign up."

"You should go. It's an exciting part of the trip."

"Wow. I guess you all get the same script."

"Who else have you been talking to?" It comes out rough, and she smiles. Jesus.

"Our waitress. Don't be jealous." I go silent, and her smile widens. "Or do."

I've already been on break too long. I need to get back to my stool. "If I ask you to go, will you?" she says, her foot with its slight sandal resting on my ankle.

"I'm not on vacation. I work." I almost tip over the table to get up, and when I get my guitar tuned and look at my audience—three couples who all look like they listened to J. D. Souther when they were Corinne's age— she's gone.

During the Jackson Browne medley, I envision the two of us. Her long, pretty hair threading into the greasy remaining hank on the back of my neck; her lovely breasts rubbing the grayish skin on my chest and back. And where would this happen? Do I pay my roommate to find another place to sleep, or take Corinne to the rope deck, which smells like tar and bilge? We could find a cozy shadow,

four feet from some other couple's cozy shadow, and ro-
mantically couple to the farting sound of the exhaust. My
voice cracks on "Doctor My Eyes," and my three couples
are looking at me closely, but no one leaves.

I wake up thinking about her and go to sleep thinking
about her. The cruise director put me on this stool because
I was old enough to trust, as he told me twice.

The next song up is "Suite: Judy Blue Eyes." I could
play something else, but I make my choice and sing a song
that was on oldies stations when I was Corinne's age, when
dinosaurs walked the earth. I'd bet two hundred bucks
that Corinne is in earshot, listening to her little pastime
sing his heart out. The woman closest to me moistens her
thin lips, leans her head on her husband's shoulder, and
goes to sleep.

Wedding Gown

Wayne is a good man. I'm lucky to get him. People keep telling me those things, as if I need reminding. He took care of his troubled sister from the time he was nineteen years old, tracking her more than once to the houses where she was shooting up and taking her back home. Wayne's youth was sacrificed on the altar of that girl. I should be grateful that a man like that wants to marry me now, when the skin under my eyes is showing lines and the legs that used to look slim and good in shorts now just look like stalks. I am grateful. But shouldn't a man have wanted a little more out of his life? Shouldn't a man have taken some time off from his mess of a sister once in a while, going out to the quarry with a few guns and friends who've been drinking? He took care of her to the day she died, and after. He was the one to wash her body for the funeral. People talked.

This is exactly why I need to wear a white dress, even if white makes me look little and washed out. Mama said I could pass for a used cotton ball. She thinks I should have a pink wedding gown. She thinks I look good in pink, which is true, but she forgets that white means something. I'm not talking about how I've had other boyfriends. Everybody in town knows that. White means respect for the tradition, and I'm trying to get this right.

I have thoughts that are not helpful. What does it mean that a man who spent ten years chasing down his sister in shooting galleries thinks that marrying me is the natural next move? Mama tells me not to say such things. I don't see why I shouldn't. Everybody who saw me pulling in to park at Monica's Bridal did.

I tried on a dress that Wayne would like—strapless, with lots of flounces on the skirt. The salesgirl had to pin it to hold it up, chattering, "Aren't you tiny! Not many of the girls who come in are so little." I looked in the mirror and saw a broomstick rising from a mound of whipped cream. "Maybe something with sleeves," I said to her, while Mama said, "You can always dye it pink." She was trying to make this a happy day. One look at her face told me she was remembering my first day of school, my first bike—the days before every room started to seem too small. Once she sent me to school in a turtleneck, and by the time I got home I'd cut out the neck with craft scissors.

I'm too old now to wear a dress designed for a twenty-year-old and Wayne must know that. He's not a fool and he

doesn't close his eyes when he looks at me. He says, "I like
a girl who's been around the block." Well, he shouldn't. He
should stand up straighter and get mad enough to snarl at
the girl he's going to marry when she comes home later
than she said she would, and drunk besides. When she
lets the guys she works with tease her that the fella she's
marrying is fussy as an old lady. Wayne shrugs and says,
"People say things," and then he asks me what I want for
dinner. Sometimes the words are right there in my mouth:
"Oh, grow a pair." He fusses at me, tucking in my scarf
and putting ChapStick on my lips so I don't have to dig
through my purse for gloss. His eyes are calm when he
does these things. He loves to tuck in my scarf.

I was barely fourteen when I went joyriding with Neil
Osterman. He was nineteen, and I knew where we were
going and what we were going to do there, and I yelled,
"Faster!" whenever he slowed down. By the time we got to
the quarry he was leaving rubber at every corner, including
the one where we'd spun out and got a grill full of green
corn. Drunk, of course, both of us, and loud, hollering as
we swung on the rope over the glassy water. People think
that Neil's drunk hands slipped on the rope and he fell
onto the boy swimming below us, but it wasn't so simple.
Neil was bombing for him and I was hanging on to Neil,
screaming either "Go! Go!" or "No! No!" I'd been drinking, too. Was that my sin, or was it the two of us, slick
and wet teenage bodies, landing on that little boy, or was
it me holding my head up after the funeral that every soul

in Winesburg seemed to turn out for? My other sin was continuing to ride with Neil until he got locked up.

Wayne knows all of this. I made sure. I don't want him coming home from the NAPA shop one day with his mouth folded back against the words he doesn't want to say to me. He wants to protect me, even now.

"Do you still love Neil? Is that it?" Mama had demanded after she heard that I turned down Wayne a second time. Of course I don't love Neil. It was Neil's house that Wayne hauled his sister out of. Without even trying I can conjure Neil's lazy sneer. He liked to blow cigarette smoke in my mouth when we kissed. No woman in her right mind loves Neil.

The salesgirl brought me another dress, with lacy sleeves that ate at my arms like a tracing of fire ants. The lace rode up in a high collar. "You won't be able to fasten this yourself, but your mama can help you," the salesgirl said. Mama looked unhappy. What did she think we were buying, a party dress? The lace pinched, so stiff I could barely bend my elbows.

"Look at you! A bride!" the salesgirl said.

In the mirror stood a girl, skinny as a needle, her skin gray underneath the stupid white lace.

"You'll be wrapped up too tight to dance at your own wedding," Mama said.

The salesgirl started to talk about alterations and Mama was saying pink, both of them chattering until I said, "Hush," as if I had a right.

"Are you crying?" Mama said.

"That's tears of joy," the salesgirl said. "I see them a lot."

"You keep thinking that," I said. My arms were too stiff at my sides to wipe my eyes, so a drop landed on the dress, spotting it and making it mine now.

Joy

These times come for no reason and too rarely, days and evenings that quiver like a bee's wing. Though I'm just sitting on my concrete back stoop, looking at my neighbor's heavy-headed peonies while a beer sweats between my hands, I envision fragrant vines draped from balconies. A breeze floats my sleeve across my arm. Nearby, a bobwhite whistles, and my skin wants to dissolve and let something pure slip free.

Today at work, I sat in my cube and proofread page after page, using the tricks I've developed to keep focused, then eventually letting the focus go; no one but me has ever cared when I missed an apostrophe. In the car on the way home, the ease of mere pleasure rose around me like water, and when I opened the car door, it spilled out in an ecstasy of nothing, of the moment I happened to be living.

Now, I thought, *Now*, the word's meaning teasingly out of reach.

This isn't the life I meant to have. I'm not saying it's worse.

When I was fourteen and my sister was nine, she nagged me until I took her to a dog show. Our parents wouldn't allow pets, so she papered the walls of her bedroom with pictures of snowy-breasted collies or Irish setters, their coats like fire, coursing through rough brush. I loved my sister; it was no hardship to go with her and look at the pretty dogs. We were allowed into the staging area where a mastiff swabbed my sister from neck to hairline in a single lick, and she hit me when I pulled her away.

The dogs panted on their grooming tables while their people buffed toenails, whitened teeth, brushed and brushed and brushed. The handlers had dog paraphernalia we could never have dreamed of: socks and headbands and jackets with their breeds on them, a car with a German shepherd painted across the hood. The lady with dachshunds wore a ball cap that had a tiny stuffed dachshund sniffing a fire hydrant on the bill. Bets nudged me when she saw it, and we had to run out of the tent because our laughter overcame us. Bets is dead now: car crash. Blood alcohol 0.120. Her pealing laughter used to unfurl all the way across the playground.

From the back of my yard a green scent drifts up, thicker than pine, a heady invitation to bees. Bets would have known the plant, its perfume a bright feather. *Nothing you love is ever gone*, some people say, and I have no idea whether that's true. She would have known the scent, I don't, and here I am opening my mouth to let the sweetness in.

I expected so many things. At sixteen I began to save items for my apartment in Madrid or Leningrad, places I believed I had a right to. A book about French painters, a yellowed comb that I thought was made of bone. My mother would hush my father when he started to laugh. "There's nothing wrong with ambition," she told him. I spent a full year sulking when I found out that my community college didn't teach Russian. My mother kept quiet two years later when I put a down payment on a one-bedroom house six blocks from where I grew up. By then she and Dad were divorced, and she was happy to have me close.

My friend Rayelle used to live across the street, and after my boyfriend and I broke up she came over at night with a six-pack and a listening ear. She would rub my shoulders until I pulled away. Rayelle made this stoop, knocking together the form and pouring the concrete so that I could have something nicer than wood plank steps coming out my back door. Pure kindness on her part. She spent an afternoon staining it, decided she didn't like how orange the stain came out, sledgehammered the whole thing and started from scratch. "I wanted it to be nice," Rayelle said. I don't know where she is now, wouldn't know where to find her, but the thing she did for me waits every day when I come out back to look for finches, which she taught me to see.

Rayelle wanted me to love her and I didn't, and she created the stoop for me anyway. Now I remember her every day. That's how love works. It took me quite a while to figure this out.

Almost a year has passed since a man has come to my house, and sometimes I feel lonely, though not often. At night a street light shines through the bright crabapple leaves in my yard, its color sizzling. Once it was enough to illuminate mating raccoons in the front yard. They uncoupled, washed their hands at the birdbath, then scurried apart without another glance. A younger me would have strained to find a meaning, but what is meaning against the rough coats and velvet hands of two raccoons humping in flat, buzzing light? They were beautiful, is what I'm trying to say.

After my sister was killed I got an Irish setter, a rolypoly puppy who grew into a lug-headed brute. He charged in any direction he pleased, no matter how I tried to restrain him, and when he got away from me he ran for miles, his tongue and tail bright pennants. I loved that dog like breath. He smiled when he saw me, and at night he'd tug off my slippers and socks, then lick my feet from ankles to toes until he'd licked the day away, a trick I never taught him. The day I had to put him down—internal bleeding, no choice—I did all right until nighttime, when

I laid on the couch, my feet covered, and tears shuddered out of me in waves.

I won't get another dog. Without any effort I recall the feel of his lavish coat, its cobwebby strands fine enough to clog the furnace filter. After he came in from a long run, his coat smelled like grass and dirt, a clean smell that I buried my nose in. The memories are on every side, and all I have to do is let them carry me. My sister and I were going to go to Africa when we were old. She wanted to see giraffes.

It comes again, that feeling that will not be commanded or contained or even named. The bobwhite, the thick scent: The pleasure of this moment obliterates thought. Quivering, shapeless emotion spills and floods out of me. I'm surprised the lizard at my feet isn't washed away.

Maybe this is grief. Who cares what we call it? Joy comes in waves, and will not hear no.

Peru

Mrs. Wright asked if I had kids and I said yes. Then she talked for ninety minutes until I broke in to tell her that the house would never get clean if I didn't get back to work. At six o'clock she said, "You're not leaving before you do the floors, are you?"

Cleaning houses means I get to work in air-conditioning, and most of my ladies are nice. Mrs. Wright is nice in her way. She's lonely, and she wants to talk, and she's got mice in her kitchen because she puts up dishes dirty. I would rather die than have somebody come into my kitchen and find mouse droppings in the cupboard, but Mrs. Wright doesn't die. She hires me.

"I really need to get somebody to help," she says, fanning her hands at the dining room table, invisible under scissors and plates and magazines and a few deflated balloons and a T-shirt and a bag of birdseed from when she had a parrot.

"That's a problem, *sí.*"

"Could you clear this?"

"If you want me to throw things away, I can do that." The birdseed has got to be at least two years old. It's gray.

"This is a big house. There's room here to put things." I smile and ignore how she twists her hands. It's best not to answer with words, because she meets words with more words. One night I didn't get home until past eight. My older son, who's wicked good at art, drew a cartoon of Mrs. Wright talking me into the floor. When Mrs. Wright is not home, I polish that floor until I can see my own face in it.

She's usually here, though, telling me things. Mr. Wright, an astronomer, left for a trip to Peru and died on a mountaintop there. Mrs. Wright and her son went to Peru to scatter her husband's ashes because, she says, he was married to his work. I've never met the son, though there are pictures around. He's handsome.

Mrs. Wright herself is jowly and heavy, with a tight permanent wave that couldn't ever have been pretty. She wraps herself in a shawl covered in pulled threads even though new clothes, tags still on them, are heaped on her bedroom floor. I stack them on the dresser so I can vacuum, and sometimes the stack gets so high it blocks the mirror. The next week, those clothes are swapped out for others, and Mrs. Wright still clutches the dirt-colored shawl. "I like neutrals. You can wear anything with a neutral. Of course, with a personality like mine, there's no need to wear bright colors. There can be too much of a good thing."

She knows herself better than I sometimes think.

She has recommended me to her friends, and I caught myself surprised that she has friends. *Linda, it's not up to you to judge*, I lecture myself. I meet her friends and find houses that don't have mouse droppings or a trail of raspberry jam drops from the refrigerator all the way to the piano. Those are houses I can clean in six hours and leave feeling proud.

A lot of weeks I never make it past Mrs. Wright's downstairs, what with the regular mess in the kitchen and her wanting to tell me about meeting her husband's parents in the Back Bay, which she describes to me. If I don't get upstairs, she cuts my pay, but I keep coming back, so who is the one at fault?

Almost every week she gives me something—a blouse, a cookie jar, half of a pound cake. I ask her repeatedly for the things I need: vacuum cleaner bags, detergent, vinegar. Heading upstairs, balancing mop and bucket and dust cloths, I say, "White vinegar. It is sold by the gallon."

"I remember the smell. If I came home from school right after my mother had cleaned the floor, my eyes would water. She would make me stay out on the porch, even when there was snow on the ground." I move to go upstairs, but Mrs. Wright is just getting started.

"I let my son come into the house whenever he wanted, no matter what he was tracking. My husband kept a tally of the rugs that were ruined, but my son knew he could always come home.

"He turned out to be one of those neat boys—isn't that funny? He wouldn't let me come into his room because he had everything the way he wanted it. Even if I promised not to touch anything, he wouldn't let me come in.

"My husband was neat, too. I knew that about him from the start. Just like he knew that I never planned to spend my life picking things up."

I clear my throat and Mrs. Wright says, "My son kept only one thing from my husband's office. I offered to ship him everything in the room, but all he wanted was a sketch our friend drew of my husband looking through a telescope. I don't know what happened to either one, telescope or friend. He would come over and drink and draw. There used to be stacks of drawings four inches deep.

"I'd say, 'Draw me,' but he wouldn't. He said that nice women didn't pose. I don't think my husband ever heard, even though our friend said it all the time. He had a little pointed beard and wasn't my type.

"I wish he had drawn me. I would like to have that sketch."

"My son could draw you." The words spill out of my mouth, and I don't think Mrs. Wright will hear me. She doesn't usually.

"When?"

For better than a month I try to pretend I never said anything, though Mrs. Wright meets me at the door and says, "Where's your son?" She forgets bills and appointments and her son's birthday. My son is the thing she remembers. The reason I submerge myself once a week in the never-ending bath of her talk is so that my son won't have to, ever.

After weeks of getting nowhere with me, she calls my house. "Is this Miguel? Your mother works for me, and she tells me that you are an artist."

It's all set up by the time I get home, and my son laughs at my flat-footed anger. "Why shouldn't I draw her? It's a good chance for me."

"I don't know what she's going to expect."

I see his own anger rise. "She expects a fine drawing. I will give it to her."

He is fifteen.

A week later we arrive at Mrs. Wright's and find that she has cleaned for us, in her way. Books and flyers and cans of beef broth have been pushed to the side of the room, and she's put a daisy in a bud vase on the coffee table beside a hat, a handful of pens, a sleeve of crackers, and a harmonica. Her smile trembles. She clasps the dirt-colored shawl over an evening gown, low at the back and front. My son arranges her on the couch, inside a square of light that makes her skin look dense, like yogurt.

"Can you talk without moving your body?"

"Don't you need me to hold still?"

"I'll tell you when I need you to stop. For now, talk to me."

Maybe no one has ever said that to her before. She takes a moment. "I used to dream of being an artist. Artists notice things, and I'm a good noticer. When I walk into a room, I see who's there, the way people are arranged. Later, when I hear that one couple's getting divorced or another one's getting married, I already know.

"That's why my husband went away. He didn't like to be watched. I said, 'What do you think marriage is?' and he said, 'Intolerable.' The things he looked at were far away, and maybe already dead.

"Your mother notices, too. She can tell when I've tried to tidy things up, and when I just said to hell with it. She can tell when I'm sad. She's like a friend."

I come once a week and bring home her check. My son's hand is busy on the page, making lots of curving lines. I'm watching both of them, the first time I've ever sat in this room.

"Now you're noticing me, and that's hard. The noticer doesn't like to be noticed. Men used to notice me, but that was different.

"Having your mother here makes things safe. My son will never let me near anything he does. He comes home once a year, for three days. He pulls at his collar as if the air in the house is too much for him. He once told me for God's sake to get rid of the star charts; Dad was not coming back. I said, 'That's why I keep them.' He thinks I'm silly."

"You aren't silly," my son says, his voice rough.

For a moment, silence rings through the room, except for the scrape of my son's pencil. Mrs. Wright says, "Can I be quiet now?"

"Yes," says my son.

The quiet stretches between us like wire. I go to the window and say, "There's a boy on a bicycle and another one on a skateboard. He's pretty good. What's that thing called, a half-pipe?" I'll keep talking until my son is finished, and the terrible looking is over.

Necropolis

This morning Ruthie Jonson died. No surprise. Her kids and grandkids are here, the youngest ones roaring down the halls and swinging from the grab bars, and the first pieces of Ruthie's furniture have already been taken. We see this played out once a month, more when the Reaper gets greedy. Normally I don't let it interrupt my walk to waterobics, but this morning I stopped and stared like I'd never seen an apartment full of trash bags before, my heart turning inside out. Taking pity, one of her busy children stopped, rested her box on her leg, and said, "Did you know her? I'm sorry. She went very peacefully."

Embarrassed by my tears, I said, "Thank you." She probably thinks her mother and I were having a sweet, old-folks love affair. Hand-holding. Ruthie and I were not especially close, and I don't know why this feels like a heart attack. I would welcome a heart attack. I live and live and live.

After lunch today I'll go up to the full-care unit and visit Syl. If it's a good day, she'll know who I am. After the bad days, I use the back staircase to get to my room and then drink a lot of whiskey.

It was Syl's idea to move here twelve years ago, when she was forty-nine and I was fifty-two. Twelve years ago, the Kenwood sounded like a smart, happy idea with its tennis courts and three different pools. We didn't have kids; we had to think ahead and take care of ourselves. Moving here didn't mean we were dying. It meant, said the salesman over the phone, that we were really living.

Christ, I believed him. Here we were, Sid and Syl, really living. We came for a tour. What has happened to those hale tennis players with the killer serves who happened to have gray hair? Syl said the Kenwood sent them back to Hollywood as soon as we signed the contract. She told jokes, back when we were in this together and realizing what we had done.

Once we were in, we were in. Might as well have heard an iron door slam shut. We signed away not just our salaries, but our retirement. Now we couldn't get out unless the place burned down, and I'm half ready to try a little arson. At night, my mouth filled with Johnnie Walker smoke, I imagine our old house. The last thing Syl and I did was shell out for cement board to replace the never-ending pain-in-the-ass siding. The new owners can rejoice in the knowledge that I, not they, paid the $20,000 to have the whole house re-clad, not just the damaged parts. "Oh no," said Sid, king of the homeowners. "Let's do it right and forget about it." On that decision alone I could have saved $12,000, enough to bankroll me at the Kenwood for an extra ten months, if I need them, and I hope I don't.

Syl's care is round-the-clock. I imagine I can hear the costs go up, like the meter in a cab. "Our first concern is her safety. You want to keep her safe, don't you?"

Once it was clear we couldn't change our minds, we were determined to make the best of things. We found the other Kenwoodians who weren't, in Syl's phrase, decrepit yet—one guy who'd suffered a head injury and had been living here since he was thirty-eight, and two couples who came here together, lived next door to each other, and took cruises together so they could play bridge. Syl's and my jokes got more and more brittle, but we were holding it together until the day I came home early from a run and surprised her in our tiny apartment, her face buried in the sweater she was using to muffle her sobs. "We're living in a *tomb*," she howled.

"Shhh. We'll work around it. We can come home from five o'clock dinner and have cocktails. We've got friends on the outside. They'll smuggle us a file in a cake." That made her giggle, at least. We had each other.

And then we didn't. One afternoon, when Syl calmly put the milk in the pantry, I realized how long I'd been not letting myself notice things—how she couldn't remember how to fasten the clasp on her necklace, the words that fell out of her brain, like *nest* and *doorbell*. On the spot I decided I would continue to cover up for her for the rest of my life, because I'd rather have sour milk and Syl than no Syl. But she left anyway. The day the director of nursing kept calling, I refused to pick up the phone. She caught up with me at dinner, and inside a month, Syl was upstairs and I was still downstairs and sometimes she called me Mort.

It took maybe half a day for the whole place to know that Syl and I were separate now, and for the first time in my life, I was a catch. "Sit with me, Sid." "Sid, can you come over here and make a fourth? We need a dummy." "Sid, are you going to entertainment hour this afternoon? There's a pianist who's going to play songs from all fifty states." They don't ask about Syl, restlessly calling out upstairs for Mort. Sometimes I tell them anyway, and they squeeze my hand.

One of them, Brenda, is persistent. She wears goggly glasses and her fingers are humped up with arthritis, but she has a throaty voice and a lazy purr of a laugh. Last night I went down for dinner—itself a rarity—and Brenda and I sat at the table well past coffee, until the staff chased us out. We were talking about the guy with the squeaky voice and the goatee who came in to teach us how to paint landscapes, and Jesus, it was a relief. This morning my next-door neighbor pointedly walked past my table "so you can save room for Brenda." If a DHS official brought the nuclear codes to my room in a locked briefcase, they'd be all over this place by lunchtime.

Brenda didn't come to breakfast, and I felt ridiculous. Then I found out about Ruthie, and I ran upstairs to see Syl even though I knew I couldn't get in between ten and eleven, when the nurses give out meds. I paused in my apartment for only long enough to pick up my car keys. The rooms were too tight. Syl said that if she turned around, she bumped into herself. I remembered her exact tone of voice, a tone I will never hear again, and allowed myself one minute to crumple with missing her. Then I went to the parking lot. Who cared where I was going? I was *going*.

"Sid! Sid-neee! Are you going out?"

"Sure am, girls. Do you need anything?"

The one who called out is round as a tomato, and adorable. Round little curls all over her round head, hands plump as a baby's. Syl couldn't stand her. Now the woman's smile is dimpled and coy. "Not me. Brenda. She's right over there." The woman gestures with her chin, and I see the group sitting on the patio, getting their fill of me charging through the parking lot as if I'm saving a damsel, as if I could save anything.

"Where are you going?" Brenda calls. Even when she's shouting, she has a nice voice.

"Jailbreak."

"All by yourself?" That's a gutsy thing to say, right there in front of her friends. She puts a lot of faith in me.

"This time," I say. "Next time, we'll see." I let the others giggle while I back out, drive for half an hour until my hands stop shaking and meds hour is over on Syl's floor. When I come back, I park in a different spot and creep up the back stairs, which might as well be my private staircase. Syl is still in bed. She doesn't even look up when I come in. With Brenda's voice rocketing around my head, it isn't enough to take her hand, the way I usually do. I strip down to my boxers and slip into bed with her, a tight fit. She doesn't protest when I put my arms around her, and eventually she starts to snore. I'm wide awake, waiting to be discovered in bed with my wife, and the scandal that comes next.

Honor

Here's what I say: My dad walked out on us after he promised he wouldn't. The last time I saw his car in our driveway, I was nine years old. By the time I was twelve and knew he wasn't coming back, I swore that I would never make a promise I didn't keep. It's easier than you think.

Here's what I say: Use your head before you open your damn mouth. Every word you say chisels your place in this world. My mother said she always knew where she stood with me, even though we only saw each other when I was between foster homes. Once, when I was mad at her, I started to say I didn't want to see her anymore, but I stopped myself. Now she comes to see me once a month, and I look forward to her visits.

When you give as many interviews as I do, you learn

what works. After ten years on the inside, I've learned to control my message. I've got the rest of my life to refine it.

In school, my teachers couldn't figure me out. Sometimes I'd hand in a report so perfect that they went home and spent hours on the Internet, trying to figure out what I'd copied it from. A lot of time I didn't hand in anything, explaining the GED I eventually got to make up for the high school diploma I didn't. It was a history teacher my senior year who pulled me aside and said, "If you say you'll do this assignment, you will, won't you?"

"Yes."

"If you do it, you can pass this class, and you can maybe graduate. You can help yourself, do you see that?"

"Yes."

"So will you?"

"No."

I know who I am, is what I'm saying. Once you know, you don't ever have to change. I'm like the rock the water swirls around.

Girls like that. Some girls. Even here, during visiting hour, I see them slide their eyes over to me when they're supposed to be looking at their boyfriend or brother. "You said you were going to write," they say to their man, and they can tell that I wouldn't let them down like that.

I told Lola, "If you need anything, I will get it for you."

"What are you, my knight in shining armor?"

"Yes."

She laughed, but she looked at me after that.

"Did you love her?" my lawyer asked. He was asking so he could craft an argument, and I didn't want to get out that way. I didn't kill Murphy because I loved Lola; I killed him because I told her I would. So I didn't answer my lawyer. He found every way he could to ask, but I muled up every time. Finally he just went with his own version anyway, making me sound like a fourteen-year-old emo cutter instead of a grown man who knew how to make his own choices. Didn't matter. I'm still looking at ninety-nine years, no parole. No Lola.

After a year here, I knew what everybody else was thinking. I knew the sights they were seeing, the songs they were hearing. I had a cellmate for a while who sang "Brown-Eyed Girl" every time he pissed. A guy named Morris who's in for armed robbery thinks about his ex-girlfriend, and another guy named Ajax thinks about getting high even though he's been clean for three years, and one of the guards thinks about Ajax's ass.

They don't know what I'm thinking, because nobody here thinks like me. When I lie awake for hours, it's not because I'm seeing Murphy with his head bashed in or even Lola kneeling on my bed wearing just a T-shirt, though that comes back to me every day whether I want it or not. I think about how she lied to me, sitting on my lap, fiddling with the button on my shirt. Murphy didn't beat her, he didn't make her turn tricks. None of that stuff. If she'd said, "I just don't like him. Can you get rid of him?" my life now wouldn't be pretty, but at least it would be seamless. Instead, my existence has a lump of untruth at the center, and it's my life, and I can't change it.

People make appointments to see me during the visiting hour. I'm interesting; I get that. People haven't seen honor before, and they look at me like I'm an endangered polar bear. I'm not pretending I'm a saint. I'm a murderer, and I say it every day to make sure I don't forget. If you think that's something no one would forget, you've never been on the inside.

Guys approach me. Nobody else has a ninety-nine-year sentence, crazy long, not even life but ninety-nine damn years, and it makes me a king. "There's somebody I want taken care of," they say. Then they say, "He's a douche. The world will be better off without him," because they've heard that I like moral arguments.

"No."

"C'mon, man. He pimps out kids." Or he steals his grandma's oxy, or he lights puppies on fire.

"No."

Eventually they get mad and threaten me, and everything gets all tense, and then they just go away and spit at me when they get the chance. Never anything worse than that. They know I'm not like them.

In ten years, exactly once has somebody almost gotten to me. A kid, only just eighteen, looking at fifteen for second-degree murder. He wanted to hear from me how the system was unfair, because if he heard it from me, it would be true. He said, "I meant to harm *nobody*. I didn't hardly know how to drive. I was scared. When I hit the accelerator the car jumped, and when I looked out the windshield, she was gone." A lot of that was probably true.

"Why'd you tell them you could drive?"

"They needed me. It didn't look hard."

"Who do you figure you let down?"

"Jesus, man. I *killed* that woman."

"You know what killed her? Your lie. Not even a planned murder that you could man up to, just a mistake from a piss-ant lie."

The kid's eyes went big, and then his dawning sneer half turned his face inside out. "Must be hard to see, looking out your own asshole all the time. You know why you got a fucking ninety-nine-year sentence?"

"Yeah. 'No remorse.'" The judge had waited after he said that, as if I was going to change my mind.

"Because you're such a goddamn prick. He was trying to teach you something, son, but your head's so far up your ass your ears are plugged."

He stormed to the other side of the rec yard to complain to Ajax, but I stayed where I was until the guard yelled for me to come in. Everything I told the kid was right. He would have to learn it for himself. A bird was whistling somewhere and I wanted to memorize its song, but it's just as well I couldn't. Fuck it. It's his song, not mine.

Bucket (1)

I thought I knew all the drawbacks to writing an advice column, the job I took on so I could keep editing Features. No holidays, no gratitude, no end to the world's misery. I'll read a letter written in pencil from a kid whose mother beats him, and the next writer will be upset because her boyfriend farts in bed.

Yesterday I read a letter from my wife, detailing her unhappiness in our marriage. She didn't sign it, but I recognized her phrases and rhythms, her way of telling me we're very wrong, we're over. I've been waiting for it. She shows me—I see—more than she thinks.

"I don't know when it stopped being happy. Now my heart is like a bucket with a hole in the bottom, and it can't hold anything anymore." Not many people but Lonnie would have come up with that. My God, she is my wife. I know how she talks.

When I come out of my office she's at the kitchen sink, washing spinach. I pull her into a hug, braving her wet hands on my back, and say, "My heart is filled with you."

"Ugh. What have you been reading?"

"Letters."

"Find letters that don't make you sound like a '70s pop song." She touches a damp finger to my eye. "Why are your eyes red?"

"Allergies?"

"There's Benadryl in the cabinet." She goes back to the spinach and for exactly two seconds I imagine saying, *I read your letter*, but my heart is like a bucket with a hole in the bottom. Lonnie is my whole life. I will do anything to make sure she is washing spinach when I come out of my office.

The letter is signed Secretly Unhappy in Omaha. Lonnie and I live in North Carolina, but this is the Internet, where everyone lives everywhere, and Lonnie has always used "Omaha" as her shortcut phrase to mean misery. When she says she spent all day in Omaha, I fix her a drink. Now she thinks she lives there.

I don't have to answer the letter. My job is to keep the column interesting, which is why I will write back to the woman with the farting boyfriend and privately, one-on-one, to the boy with the pencil. Normally I don't bother with the-magic-is-gone letters, but this is Lonnie, and she is reaching out to me, and it might be my last chance. I've seen the moments when her face turns wistful, when she thinks I don't see and the light filling the yard is heavy and drowsy and as gold as honey. It isn't easy to turn my back on her and return to my office.

Dear Omaha,

He doesn't know how to help. Please give him a chance.

I'm leaning so close that my nose almost grazes the computer screen. From behind me Lonnie says my name and I jump and cry out and turn around all at once, and she says, "What are you looking at, porn?"

"I don't. I wouldn't."

"Cool your jets, Dudley Do-Right. Dinner's on." Her look is pure sitcom, the exasperated wife navigating around her husband, Captain Clueless.

"Let's have wine."

"I have book club tonight. Bad night to front-load."

"Skip book club. We'll drink wine and listen to bossa nova."

"You're funny. Pasta's getting cold."

Dear Omaha,

Do you spend time together? Does he look, really look at you?

Lonnie's hair used to be black as ink, but gray started to thread in when she was in her thirties. "I'm not going to dye it," she said, as if I'd ever suggest such a thing. Her hair now is the color of steel wool. When morning light turns it gold, she looks like a Renaissance angel.

"What," she says.

"Nothing. You're beautiful."

"Have you been hitting the wine without me?"

"I do not drink without you. Much."

After she leaves for book club, I look at the letter again. "Everything we say to each other, we've said before. I can hear our conversation all day long without him ever being in the house."

If the letter writer weren't my wife, I would respond, *You need to tell him what would be exciting for you*, but I've been in this business long enough to know that the answer is "Another man." I write, *Do you love him at all?* Then I delete it because the question scares me.

In two months Lonnie and will celebrate our eighteenth anniversary. Eighteen years is longer than I've done anything else, including this advice column. It's enough time for wistfulness to grow, the putting-away of golden dreams. Lonnie thinks it does no good to talk about these things. O, my girl. Thinking about her gets me to call up phrases I would never think otherwise, sweetly old-fashioned ones like *dear heart*. Tonight, while she is at book club, I learn that the thought of being here without her brings me to my knees.

By the time she gets home, I've got wine in an ice bucket in the living room, crackers and cheese on a plate. "Wow," she says. "I thought you'd be watching the play-offs. I had a glass of wine at book club."

"You can have another one with me."

She collapses into the armchair, where I can't sit next to her, but she accepts the glass I hand her. "Celia led the discussion. That woman is dumb as a box of hair."

"Was Dave around?"

"Not a chance. This was an estrogen event."

"I was thinking while you were gone." I mean to take just a sip of wine, but I wind up with a slug that takes a second to go down. Lonnie's face is a little tired, a little tipsy. Dear heart. "It's been nineteen years."

"Eighteen, Einstein. Almost eighteen."

"Nineteen since I proposed. To the day."

"Let me guess. You got a letter about a proposal that sent you back to reading your old diaries."

"No." The lamplight catches on hairs clinging to the sleeves of her blue sweater. Her dimples hover; she's waiting for me to make a joke. She has always loved my jokes. "I just remember. I didn't do it right then."

She straightens up, and her eyes flick nervously. "If you take a knee, I'm leaving the room."

"Shouldn't I have done that then, Lonnie? Shouldn't I have told you that I didn't want to live without you? Shouldn't I have said more than 'Um, what if we got married?'"

"It worked, didn't it?" Her face is pinched with panic now, but it is brightly alive. I can see myself in her eyes—imploring, yes, but surprised. Now it's her turn with the mouthful of wine. "You don't need to do this."

"But I want to do it. With all my heart." New, fresh

blood seems to be pouring through me, every inch of my skin is sparkling, and I want her to feel as happy as I do.

"If I beg you to stop, will you?"

I think it over, assessing her panic-stricken face. "No."

Bucket (2)

Eddie comes in the door with his nightly smile already in place. Before we got married, I never knew whether he would come home happy, paid, and reaching for me, or whether he'd roar in like a comet, burning everything he touched. Or whether he would come home at all. It was thrilling, the not-knowing. Every word he said was singed a little at the edges from the rage he carried everywhere.

I don't know where the rage went. "Eddie seems happy," my mother says. Dinner is over and Eddie's stretched out in a recliner, his pants unbuttoned. I wink at him, but he's looking at the TV.

"Livin' the good life," I say, beating him to it. Later he will tell her that he wishes I'd inherited her cooking as well as her good looks. She will say that she did her best with me and he shouldn't blame her. They will laugh and agree that I'm a stubborn one. I could move to Mars and not miss one syllable.

I met him when I was waiting tables at Denny's. I kept saying I was going to try college, but there were always reasons not to start. "Placeholder job," my parents said. "Job," I said. Eddie came into the restaurant, good-looking, and ordered coffee. I brought him pie, too. He said, "You always this nice?"

"No."

"What are you doing this weekend?" Turned out I was going shooting with him. We went out to a field he knew where somebody'd set up bales, and he handed me a semiautomatic.

"Where are you going to be?" I said, scared to death, like the gun was going to turn itself around and shoot me.

He slipped behind me, stretched his arms alongside mine, and pressed tight. "Right here. Keep your eyes steady, and squeeze the trigger when you're ready." The sound of the first shot coursed through me like lava, so I shot again. We stayed there all afternoon, him pressed to my back, till I had shot all the ammo he brought.

"Sorry. I didn't mean to be greedy."

"I like it. You liked it."

The air between us burned. That night, in the light from the dashboard, he looked about seventeen, though he was twenty-three. Now, eight years later, he looks forty-five. What's the difference? Marriage. Me.

So I wrote to Ask Kevin, even though nobody else

in his column had a problem like mine. What was I supposed to say? *It's too easy. I want the man I married, not the man I'm married to.* I settled for *My heart feels like a bucket with a hole in the bottom*, which is fancy but gets at what I mean.

The second the letter went out I felt stupid and guilty. I know the rule: Don't expect anybody to boo-hoo about luck that looks good to them. When Eddie came home I wrapped myself around him like a vine. "Damn. Hold your horses, woman." He hung up his jacket and poured himself a glass of water. My guilt drained away along with every ounce of desire. I want to love him, and would settle for liking him. *My husband*, I think, and feel my heart, that bad bucket, gurgle and go empty.

This is life, not an ongoing never-ending date. But there's nothing wrong with wanting to be surprised every once in a while.

If Ask Kevin ever writes back, I'm ready for the question about other men. I, Ask Kevin, have seen the fitness center at the Cherry Hills Holiday Inn where I used to work, the comb-overs and paunches looking up hopefully every time the hotel employee comes in with fresh towels. Ask Kevin, I'm not an idiot. I am well acquainted with the options in Omaha. I'm asking you how to fix my leaky heart so that it will hold contentment and affection. Why do those words always sound like second-best?

Eddie didn't tell me he loved me until after we were married. My friend Carisse told me it was a bad sign. "He's withholding. He won't give you emotional support. How often does he go down on you?"

She asked me that all the time. Her boyfriend never did, and she was convinced every other girl was getting more.

Carisse had it wrong. Eddie went down on me a lot, but he made me wait. The waiting was almost intolerable, and glorious. It was like sex. Everything was like sex. Now he says "I love you" every night, obedient as a wind-up dog. I never asked him to.

"He's a good man," says my father with obvious surprise. This means that Eddie hasn't come to him for a loan, unlike my two brothers-in-law. At holiday dinners, Eddie and Dad sit in the living room. I'm the one who disappears with the naughty brothers-in-law and comes to the table with dilated eyes and a throat filled with giggles. Eddie rubs my leg under the table. My heart could not be any emptier.

He didn't change. He tells me this with bewilderment when we fight—that is, when I pick a fight, which I'm good at. I thought a guy who picked up the Denny's waitress and took her shooting was an outlaw. He was just relieved that I didn't expect him to take me out to dinner.

It was good at first, I wrote Ask Kevin. *Does somebody have to be at fault?* Because if somebody does, Ask Kevin doesn't need to bother telling me who's the guilty party. I married Eddie to be bad, and he married me to have somebody to come home to, and how are those pieces supposed to fit together? When he gently holds my hand, I squeeze his, both hoping and fearing he'll understand that I wish he wouldn't be so gentle.

The day he proposed, he drove for a long time without saying anything. I studied the tight line of his mouth and ran my fingernail lightly along the leg seam of his jeans until he said, "Don't do that." He drove us over to Seward County, where we could look up into the tops of cottonwoods and silver maples, the branches weaving into a green roof that could hide us. He said, "A hundred years ago, anybody who came here could kill himself and his body would never be found. Or he could kill somebody else. No one would be the wiser."

The moment between us grew hot and ripe. I didn't think he was going to kill me. I just didn't know what he was going to say next, maybe "I killed a man" and maybe "I'm hungry." He said, "Let's get married," and I would have said yes a thousand more times.

Isn't that love, Ask Kevin? If you even know. If you, with your fancy job, have ever dropped to your knees out of pure want, and wish you could do it again.

Cliché

The house would depress Jesus. My ten-year-old son walked in once right after I started working there and right away saw the nail pops and badly cut drywall; some of the outlet plates don't even cover the holes. Seven hundred grand, which is what it costs to get bad drywall in Orange County.

The homeowner saw an eighteen-foot ceiling and a bonus room. She didn't notice that the loft looked into a wall. She didn't see the corner that dropped away in the living room, probably from a dissolving foundation. She didn't even see the windows clouding up because they were installed wrong and now the seal was broken. She was not smart. Which was good, because she didn't see me watching her.

I'd heard the stupid jokes and I knew the clichés,

which never applied to me. No client ever slipped off her robe when she saw me coming. I never had to explain to my wife a strange pair of panties in my pocket. I didn't do that shit, and neither did other contractors I knew, though we laughed over beers at Hollywood's ideas of our lives. I didn't like myself for knowing where she was whenever I was in her house. I didn't like remembering the music she listened to. I didn't like my eyes for noticing the glints of blond in her hair illuminated by the light coming through the crappy window.

"Where do you want the outlet to go?" With other clients I found out about kids and vacations. I said, "Are you planning to stain this trim?"

She held up two paint samples. "What do you think?"

I couldn't stop myself—I said, "That one," because the other one would look like chalk, and it was important to me that she live in a nice house. At night I thought of her and twitched with the need to save her from bad choices.

When I got home I checked my son's homework and snaked the bathtub drain. I became Superhusband since taking this job, and my wife smiled when I walked through the door. I wondered how much quiet deceit a marriage could contain.

At work the homeowner asked me to recode her garage-door opener. There was a manual; all she had to do was read it. Instead she stood next to me while I read, then trailed me to the garage while I instructed her to punch in her new code. "Don't tell me what it is," I said.

"Silly. I trust you."

"You want to keep the information to yourself."

Her blouse was buttoned wrong, and it was unbelievably hard not to reach out and fix it.

"Put this manual someplace safe. If you want to change the code, it will tell you how to do it."

"If I want to change the code, I'll call you."

A few times I stayed late, hoping I could meet her husband. It would have helped to shake the man's hand, but he worked late paying for that shithole house, and his wife was alone a lot. She wasn't alone. She was with me.

I was hired to work on an addition. Once the addition was finished, she kept finding new jobs for me, and when those threatened to end, I drew her attention to a crack that ran all the way around the downstairs bathroom.

"Is it dangerous?"

"Only if you want your house to keep standing."

Her face was a cartoon of confusion and sweet alarm. This was what Betty Boop would look like if she was talking to her contractor. I would look like the wolf.

I went back to that house yesterday. It's brown now, and the trees make it look less crude. Kids' toys are scattered on the driveway; either she's a grandmother or she sold the place. I heard that she and her husband split, but I don't know whether that's true. Even now I can make myself gasp a little at the idea of her available.

I got out of that job without ever kissing her. All my crazy, pent-up need went into the next job, Marcie, who broke up my marriage. She and I lasted three years. Pretty good, for how these things go. Three years after that my son started to talk to me again. Eventually we pasted the edges back together. He comes and sees me now sometimes just because he wants to.

I live in a house south of town. It isn't much, but the land is good, and I keep the place clean. I could bring a woman there without feeling too bad. Most of the time I don't bring women there. That fire burned itself out after the divorce, after Marcie, after I lived through all the destruction that I knew I was bringing on myself, and couldn't stop. Didn't stop. Of course I could have.

This house I used to work on looks pretty good now. Somebody's keeping it up. The gutters look good, and the roof, and the mulch is pulled away from the foundation. If I look at it like this, from the street, it's a solid house that could hold any number of good lives. If I tilt my head just a little, I can feel the edges of the old thrill. That's all it takes, that little tilt.

Nutcracker

Mom has been playing that awful, plinky music all morning. Like Grandma's, her face is smeared with excitement, and if they really want to do something for me, they can take themselves to the Nutcracker and let me stay home.

"I remember the first time I went to see it," Grandma says. She wants to pull me into her lap, but she settles for stroking my hair. She used to have a cocker spaniel. "I was just your age. The music, the costumes—I'd never seen anything so beautiful. I dreamed about it for weeks afterward."

"You're still dreaming of it," I say, which isn't supposed to be funny.

"You've heard the music in ballet class," Mom says. Her voice is part coax, part threat. "You know some of the dances."

"No, I don't."

"You were a waltzing flower."

"We didn't do the real steps, we just used the music. We're not good enough to do the real dances."

"It will be exciting to see the real dances, and girls just like you doing them."

Not just like me. Girls who don't get dizzy and fall down on pirouettes, girls who don't clunk in their toe shoes. Girls who, if they aren't performing, start pestering their mothers in August to get tickets to the Nutcracker.

"I wanted so much to be Clara," Grandma is saying. "To dance with the Nutcracker Prince! Oh, I used to dream of it."

"Clara is an idiot."

"Here it comes," Mom says to Grandma. "I didn't think she would start with the ugly until she was a teenager."

"Serves you right," Grandma says to her.

"She *is* an idiot." Tears start to crowd my voice, and that pisses me off. If we're going to have this stupid conversation, I don't want to blubber. "A spooky old man comes into the party and pays her a lot of attention and keeps touching her hair, and then he gives her a special toy. And nobody says anything, they just keep dancing around, the stupid snowflakes and soldiers and flowers, when he's going to take her away and *hurt her*. And *nobody's listening*." The tears are everywhere now, and the snot, and Mom is literally holding me by the wrist while she and Grandma can't stop laughing.

"You shouldn't be scared," Grandma says, dabbing at her laugh-tears. "Good grief, child, it's ballet. It's *pretty*."

"It isn't pretty. It's spiky, like knives coming at you."

"Where does she get this?" Grandma says.

Mom shrugs. "TV? We'll be going along fine and then suddenly something will go wrong and—well." "Well" is me frantically trying to break away from her grip, which keeps getting tighter. "Annabelle, stop. Just stop. You're too old to throw a tantrum."

"At school my teachers tell me to name danger when I see it."

"Well, they aren't talking about the Nutcracker," Mom says.

"This wouldn't happen if you sent her to church school," Grandma murmurs.

"Not the time, Ma."

When things are better, it's Mom and me against Grandma. Mom makes fun of Grandma for not knowing how to use her phone, and I show her new apps and settings while she tells me to slow down. Mom and I laugh. But now it's the two of them bearing down on me, waiting for the shell to shatter.

"Honey, smile. You're so pretty when you smile."

Grandma's not as tall as Drosselmeyer, the man who gives Clara the nutcracker, but like him she grins too much and comes close enough for me to cough from her powdery perfume.

"Fuck you." I've been saving it up. Mom is shocked

enough to loosen her grip and I'm out the door. She closes the door behind me. It's cold, and I don't have a coat.

Who thinks that snowflakes are anything like ballerinas? Stinging pellets shoot through my socks. I tuck my fists under my arms and keep half running, half sliding away from the warm house. Mom and Grandma are probably still laughing, the way you do when you know you're going to win.

At the end of our backyard is a cruddy drainage ditch that doesn't get enough water to wash out the rags and plastic and food wrappers that slide down the hill. Stuff just collects. My friend Marnie said she found a syringe but I don't believe her. She's too prissy to sift through trash for something as small as a syringe, and she never showed it to me. She came to school looking sleepy and said she'd shot up, but I don't believe that, either.

It's ugly down here, but the sides of the ditch stop the wind and it's too cold to stink. I smooth out two plastic bags and sit on them, pretending I don't mind the cold that flares across my butt. Everybody knows what happens to girls out by themselves in the snow, so I wrap my arms tight around my legs and wait for a man to show up.

No man materializes. Aside from the shadows turning purple, nothing happens at all. I hear a door open, and Mom calls, "Annabelle? You made your point. Come back in now." In a different neighborhood, she'd be worried.

I'm shuddering more than shivering, heavy waves running over me. Mom and Grandma agree that if there's a delicate way to do anything, I won't find it, another big laugh line. By the time I stand up, my feet are so numb that I'm walking like Bigfoot. I trudge up to the road and stick out my thumb for a minute, but that feels fake, so I just walk, clumsy on numb feet. Ten minutes? Fifteen? I'm about halfway to the railroad crossing when the police car pulls up next to me.

The lecture is everything I know it will be: danger, risk, do I have any idea. I'm rubbing my feet. He takes me back home, where Mom and Grandma are drinking Cokes and watching TV. "Missing something?" he says, pushing me ahead of him.

Mom looks at Grandma. "What do you think, Ma? We missing anything here?"

"I can't think what," Grandma says.

The policeman has barely stopped laughing when he looks at me with his teacher face. "Don't let me hear about you taking off again. Next time you won't be so lucky." Mom pinches my shoulder, which keeps me from being nice.

"That's the plan," I say.

Stingers

Bob gunned the Pontiac the whole way here—he drives aggressively when he's mad. Tonight he was complaining in advance about Lance's liquor, his record collection, his insistence that we all take off our shoes at the door, which is strange but makes dancing more fun. "He wants to make sure we all know how nonconformist he is," Bob said, yanking the Pontiac around a corner so the tires squealed.

"We don't have to go," I said.

He glanced at me, then squeezed my knee. "You're so funny."

Since we got engaged he's been more handsy, squeezing and rubbing my arms and waist, and I don't need to be a mind reader to know he's counting down the nights till our wedding. He wants to make me happy. He gave me the pearl necklace I wear when we go out.

Lance meets us at the door wearing a red plaid sports coat. "Welcome!" he says, and Bob says, "What's that you say? I can't hear you over your jacket." Everybody laughs. Bob's a card.

Lance has mixed up a pitcher of stingers, and Bob says, "What's the matter? Run out of gin?"

"I like stingers," I say. "This is a nice change."

"Better watch out, Bob," Lance says. "She's already getting feisty."

"She'll learn." Bob pulls me to his side and runs his thumb over my hip.

Lance is throwing the party all by himself—to prove, Bob said, that he can. Lance and his wife separated a month ago, and now everybody at their company has an opinion about who did the cheating. Since Bob and I are together, I hear the gossip, but my job, Bob says, is not to talk about it. Bob does, of course. He's certain that Lance has a nonconformist girlfriend on the side. "Too bad she couldn't do anything about his taste in clothes!" What Bob doesn't see is how thin Lance has become, and the way his face loses its shape when he thinks no one is looking.

"Shrimp!" I say, looking at the coffee table. The ashtrays are already little pyramids of shrimp tails and cigarette butts. "Lance, you're treating us like royalty."

"What are friends for?" he says.

"Didn't help yourself to the petty cash, did you?" Bob says just as the record comes to an end, and his words blare through the smoky room. I don't think I'm the only one to see the weariness in Lance's smile, but he just goes to change the record. He's playing bossa nova, and I hear Bob explaining to the men beside him that he himself likes Al Hirt, which he certainly does.

Carol, married to Pete in Receivables, asks me how the wedding plans are coming. This is nice of her. The wives don't have to talk to me yet; I've still got six months of college to go, and I'm not quite baked, as Bob likes to say. "We're still fussing over the guest list. I wanted to keep things small, but Bob has so many friends."

"He's social. I wish Pete had a little more Bob in him. Pete's idea of a great weekend is a ball game on the radio."

"Hey. That's my idea of a great weekend, too," says Lance, materializing with a drink for me. He's drenched in English Leather, and his smile is full of effort. "How about you, Connie? What does Bob need to do to please you?"

I can tell from the angle of Bob's head, ten feet away, that he's listening to us. "Weekends in Paris are always nice." This gets a good chuckle from the group; the only one to keep looking at me is Lance, who says, "He should take you."

"He will, one day."

"He should take you now."

"Lance, sweetheart, have you been drinking your own cooking?" says Carol. Her solicitous arm turns him toward the group. Alone with my stinger, I examine the magazines on his coffee table, a trick I learned many cocktail parties ago. *Life* has a cover picture of Gordon Cooper holding his helmet; even in a space suit, he's handsome. Bob's insecure about his looks, and I'm not about to gush over an astronaut in front of him. Still, I have eyes.

"Desafinado" grinds to an end, the record so scratched that I can hear every night that Lance sat up late, his marriage crumbling around him, and listened to soft, sad music. He's carrying a tray of glasses back to the kitchen; all he needs is an apron. On the drive home, Bob and I will laugh.

When Lance comes back out of the kitchen, I hold up my arms. "Got a dance for a girl?"

"Thought you'd never ask," he says.

The song is whispered and sultry, and Lance is a good enough dancer to make me look good, even with both of us still holding our drinks. After Bob and I are married I can tell Lance that he has soft eyes. He murmurs, "You're too good for him," the kind of flirting these fellows always do. It saves them the trouble of thinking up a new line. Then he says, "We'll have to be careful."

"Whoops!" I shriek, my stinger going all over Lance's awful sports coat. He ought to look angry, but he just steps back, and now we're ten safe feet away from each other.

"That's my girl. Can't hold her liquor!" Bob says.

"Cheap date!" says Pete.

"They all start that way," Bob says, and everybody

laughs. They didn't laugh so readily before he was promoted, but he'll always be the manager now. I touch my necklace and smile at Carol, who turns away. I'm not quite baked.

Bob's wrong about me; I have a good head for liquor. He's the one who's swaying a little at the door, and I'll cross my fingers all the way home. Lance finds our coats in the bedroom and rests mine gently over my shoulders. "Good night, beautiful," he says, making sure Bob can hear him. His fingers are light as breath on my neck. I move just barely away from him. Careful, careful.

Teeth

My car didn't want to start this morning—Dan says it's the distributor cap—so I was late getting to work, and the first patient was already in the chair. Dr. Ross will be mad at me when he has time, and his assistant, Marnie, will say, "The receptionist is supposed to greet people," using her slow voice. This patient must have been a walk-in, probably waiting at the door when Dr. Ross arrived. Meaning a mess in the mouth. Meaning no insurance. Meaning four or five wadded bills pulled from a pocket. Later today my job will be to start the quiet conversation about payment plans. "You know what to say to these patients. They listen to you," Marnie says, pretending she isn't looking at the hole in my mouth where a tooth should be. This is steady work, with air-conditioning, and I make out the vacation schedules and give myself twelve days a year.

Marnie put the patient in the far examining room and turned up the music, but there's no missing the moans, and I wonder how long this woman has been living with the pain beating like a hammer in her head. We get one or two a month like this, people who've put off and put off the visit and who hope oil of clove can combat an infection that's already blown a hole right up through the sinus cavity. I lost my best aunt that way. The undertaker had to puff up the side of her face with cotton balls.

"I don't mean to lecture," Marnie likes to say to Dr. Ross, "but *damn.*"

I'm listening to Dr. Ross's steady voice, and I can make out the speech about saving the viable teeth and about bridges, how teeth are a structure meant to last a lifetime, but they require maintenance. Does he know that everybody in town calls him Dr. Dollar? Probably.

Then there's another voice, a man's. Usually Marnie's good at keeping family from going back with the patient. Nobody wants to see their loved one's rotten, stinking tooth ripped from whatever is left of the bone, but this man must have bulled past her. I'm curious enough to stroll back and glance in at him—big, handsome, expressionless, maybe forty. He and his wife aren't tweakers. They're probably carrying cavities that started when they were eight years old. "Take them all out," he's saying to Dr. Ross, who winces. Marnie frowns at me to get back to the desk, but I can still listen from there.

"Mr. Poole, she still has several viable teeth. I can't remove them. That would be malpractice."

"I live with her and see her cry from the hurt. You don't. Get 'em out of there."

"We can make things better. Once we remove the teeth that are destroyed, just one bridge—"

"Listen." He could have sounded threatening, but the man just sounds tired. He must have known what to expect, coming to Dr. Dollar. "Last night our boy was sick and she couldn't even hold him because when he moved her head swam. I had to pull him away."

"That's the one tooth where the infection is worst."

"And then it will be the next one. Everybody in my family has took them out. She can get dentures."

"Dentures are not an inexpensive . . ."

"You think I don't know that?"

Not one sound from the woman. From thirty feet away and around two corners I can tell that she's used to having her husband talk for her. I can also imagine Dr. Ross staring at the light fixture and Marnie pushing back her expensive hair, red this month, and pulling on a pair of gloves over her first pair of gloves; the woman's mouth is probably a riot of bacteria.

I run my tongue along my gum line, checking for breaches. Sometimes at night I don't stop flossing until blood comes, going around and around the space where 4, my second bicuspid, used to be. That one went before I started working for Dr. Dollar and, Dan says, decided to play with the team—he means the fluoride rinses, which he thinks are silly. I nag him to floss, but he shrugs and goes to bed. At least he brushes now.

I wanted to get a false tooth once I'd been working ninety days and my insurance kicked in, but Marnie and Dr. Ross said no. "The deductible's costly on your salary, and really, you don't need it. Your other teeth are good," Dr. Ross said. "We could whiten them, if you want."

"But you don't need to," Marnie said fast, before I could agree. "You're good just as you are. People see you and they know this is a place they can come, where there'll be people like them."

"And not like you," I snapped, and she had the grace to blush. Single woman making $2,500 a month, she thinks she has a hard time because she has auto payments. Let's discuss Dan's mother, moved into our living room after her house was robbed down to the studs. Or Dan himself, hands so stiff from arthritis that he can barely open a jar. Nobody's brought up whitening again, though Marnie gets hers done every two months like church.

Now the man says, "You ain't the only dentist. We can get somewhere else."

After a pause, Dr. Ross says, "I'll take out the worst ones. After that, we can take impressions for temporary dentures that she can wear until the permanent ones are made."

"We're not doing none of that."

"I'm sorry, but this is the best we can do. We'll need at least a month. We'll try to get the order expedited."

I'll bet it was "expedited" that set the man off. I can hear him lean forward, closing the space between him and Dr. Ross. "Listen. I took off work today. I'll get cut eighty-five bucks for that. She took off work, and may not have a job tomorrow. We are here today."

A long minute passes before Marnie comes up front. I'm already pulling out the form. When no patient is in earshot, we call it the Don't Sue Us, a joke that's funny if you're not the one who will have to explain to Mr. Poole how he can't blame us for pain, or bleeding, or infection, or a bad outcome, a phrase that covers anything from soreness to death. Marnie reminds me every month or so that it's the most important part of my job. Of course it is. It keeps her from having to have an actual conversation with the portion of our clientele who don't arrive in cars with good paint jobs and who really watch the TV in the waiting room.

"Also," Marnie says, "could you reschedule Mrs. Toland's appointment for this afternoon? Any time next week would be fine." Eighty-five if she's a day, Mrs. Toland has to move heaven and earth to get her daughter to bring her in, when she talks to us about the old dentist, the one before Dr. Ross, the one she liked.

Before I call her I enter Mr. Poole's information into the computer, transposing digits in both his phone number and his address. This way his credit might not get dinged when the bills for $500 worth of extractions go unpaid. It's worked before. Then I bring him a bottle of water. He looks at the bottle and looks at me and I smile, automatically covering my gap. He's tan and muscled. Anywhere but here he would turn heads. I say, "It's all we have on offer. Dentist's office."

"I've been getting the message."

"There are machines downstairs. Can I get you anything else?"

He snorts softly. "Got a miracle handy?" Closing his eyes, he leans back, his features scrubbed of everything but fatigue. He will be sitting back there for better than an hour, feet planted, making sure that the worst of his wife's pain is taken away. Dr. Ross will get maybe sixty bucks. Out front, I wipe Marnie's upcoming whitening appointments off the schedule, assign myself a sick day tomorrow, and practice smiling so my missing tooth shows, so Mr. Poole knows who he's talking to.

Prayer

Because you promised to be with me even to the end of time. Because you told me to be still and know who you are. Because it was said you would lead me through the shadow of the valley of death and take away my fear, but I still have my fear. *Because you promised me repose.*

Because I have not been made new. Because I still reach for the glass every morning. Because you promised me joy. Because you make promises you don't keep.

Because when I ask where the rent money will come from, you say, "How glorious is the daybreak." When I remind you that my savings have dwindled to pennies, you say, "It is good that there is music." Because you expect me to be a mystic, but did not make me a mystic. I have clung to your promises until my hands ache. When the day comes that I open them, I am pretty sure I'll discover they are empty.

Because destruction might pave the way to salvation, but salvation can be destroyed again. You have lifted me up, as you promised. But salvation has set me swinging on a trapeze, looking for hands to clasp. Because those hands might come, and they might not. Because if I am left to fall, everyone will understand that being left breathless and broken on the tent floor was good for me. Because everything you do or don't do is good for me.

Because you promise to break and remake us when we go wrong, and because you have made us so that we don't want to be broken, and we often go wrong. Because last night I brought home a woman who smelled like olives and whose touch on my wrist made my arm feel electrified. Because I wanted to shout in gratitude that there was such a woman, you made her, and I met her. Because she went home with me, and because we were shaking so hard when we touched each other that we both dropped our glasses—which held nothing but Sprite, a point you should appreciate.

Because she is married, which I knew right after she looked around the bar, then looked at me and said, "Neither one of us should be here."

I told her the truth: "I come here every night. If I can't sit in a bar, then I can't go to parties, and then I won't be able to go to restaurants. I won't be able to let people come

---

to my apartment. Before long, I'll be curled up all alone, and then the only solution will be to come here."

"So it's all about choice?" she said.

"Mostly," I said.

"Then I am choosing to sit with you," she said. "Move over."

Because you created choice. Because life is an endless succession of choose, choose, choose, and eventually we're going to choose wrong, and then discover you waiting at the threshold of that wrong choice. Even till the end of time. Because your sure patience might be the most threatening promise ever made.

Because I've been alone so long—because I was supposed to be alone, and being alone was good for me. Because I have been purified by solitude. Because you also created a sense of humor, which has come in handy. Because I laughed when we dropped our glasses, and so did she. I laughed again when I pulled her against me, and she did not laugh then.

Because my thoughts run to her like water racing downhill. Because she is married. Because she sang along with the song on my radio, and knew every word. Because she knows how to sing harmony. Because when she was little, she had a dog named Skipper. Because she is married.

Because you are so elusive on some subjects, and so icily clear on others. Because your forgiveness comes with riders, like the contracts that used to come and that I pretended to read, but rarely get past the third *whereas*. Because, you will say, you forgive any truly penitent heart, but that penance must nonetheless be enacted. Because I am not penitent. Because I want to call her. Now. And now.

Because her husband's name is Gary, and I have never met a Gary I didn't like. Because she did not want to tell me about the accident, but I kept asking until she told me. Because people can fall from rooftops while doing nothing more exceptional than cleaning gutters. Because home maintenance can create a man who does not remember his wife's name, but remembers how to fumble for her waist when she passes with a pile of laundry. Because at first she leaned into his grasp, thinking that his body might remember her even if his mouth could not produce her name. She leaned into him until she couldn't lean anymore. She did not tell me this. She fell silent, her hard gaze directed at the table and her mouth soft. Because you gave her a soft mouth.

Because comfort is sometimes offered, and is a kindness. Because my heart swelled at her sorrow. Because you gave me a heart that would do that.

Because I have entered a room with only one exit, a room you allowed me to find. Because I can see the future so clearly it might as well be my past. Because people who come together out of famished need gnaw each other to pieces. It will be no time before I resent her for my helplessness before her need, as she will resent me. Because you have made the journey from joy to weariness a trapdoor drop, and because the early claims on us are the ones that endure. Because I am rushing toward my own sadness and hers, and I will not even slow my step.

Because you will be with me in my suffering. Because suffering is what you made us for. My heart will break and I will turn to you, because you are the only one to turn to. Because you made the rules. Because in the heartbreak I already feel, you will be saving me. I do not want to be saved. Because my desires do not matter. Because when the time comes, I will be looking for you, the last one I want to see.

Acknowledgments

"America" originally appeared in *American Short Fiction*; "Ava Gardner Goes Home" in *The Sewanee Review*; "Before" in *A Very Angry Baby: The Anthology*; "Breaking Glass," "Dogs," "Happiness," and "Priest" in *Image*; "Cat," "Comfort (1)," "Comfort (2)," "Job," "Rock and Roll," and "Sympathy" in *The Georgia Review*; "Cliché," "Pariah," "Pebble," and "The Tenth Student" in *The Cincinnati Review*; "Compliments," "L.A.," and "Love" in *Great Jones Street*; "Fat" and "Haircut" in *Blackbird*; "Hello from an Old Friend" in *Tin House Flash Friday*; "Hope" in *Ploughshares*; "Management" and "Teeth" in *Kenyon Review Online*; "Nutcracker" in *Five Points*; "Prayer" as "A Statement from the Defense" in *St. Katherine Review*; and "Wedding Gown" as "Deanne Stovers" in *Winesburg, Indiana*.

This book would not have been born without the

steady help and support of Gail Hochman, to whom I owe more than I can count. Thank you to the miraculously patient Jody Kahn. Deep and happy thanks to Jack Shoemaker and the marvelous Counterpoint team—Wah-Ming Chang, Yukiko Tominaga, Megan Fishmann, Sarah Grimm, Hope Levy, Jennifer Kovitz, Katie Boland, and Jennifer Alton. You all made it fun.

I owe particular and heartfelt thanks to readers who helped me with these stories, particularly Anna McGrail, Debie Thomas, Kathleen Blackburn, and Alyssa Sumpter. Jamie Lyn Smith Fletcher saved me from myself more times than I can count. And my husband, Andrew Hudgins, read and reread, helped and rehelped, and kept me and the book alive through the bad parts.

ERIN McGRAW, born and raised in Southern California, lived and taught for many years in the Midwest before retiring to rural Tennessee with her husband, poet Andrew Hudgins, and her dogs. She has written six previous books—three novels and three collections of stories—along with essays and occasional journalism. Find out more at erinmcgraw.com.